"How often do you do this?" B... beating like a drum. He didn't even know if he was asking the right questions. "Do you do this with the kids in the house?"

"No!" Ashley squeaked. "It's not as if Regina is a guy or anything, so technically it's not cheating." She reached out for his hand. "It's nothing for you to worry about or even think about. I swear it won't ever happen again, and I've never done this with the kids in the house."

Brandon backed out of her reach. His mind couldn't grasp the fact that his wife of eight years was telling him that catching her in bed with another person wasn't cheating.

He felt betrayed. He felt incredulous. He was almost speechless with the thousand and one high volts of emotions rocking through him.

"I understand that you are shocked and furious but I am sorry," Ashley said in a panicked rush.

He was not responding and she was wringing her hands guiltily. "I'll make it up to you, I swear."

ON THE REBOUND

BRENDA BARRETT

On The Rebound

A Jamaica Treasures Book/December 2014

Published by Jamaica Treasures
Kingston, Jamaica

978-976-8247-24-7
Jamaica Treasures
P.O. Box 482
Kingston 19
Jamaica W.I.
www.fiwibooks.com

ALSO BY BRENDA BARRETT

ABOUT THE AUTHOR

Books have always been a big part of life for Jamaican born Brenda Barrett, she reports that she gets withdrawal symptoms if she does not consume at least two books per week. That is all she can manage these days, as her days are filled with writing, a natural progression from her love of reading. Currently, Brenda has several novels on the market, she writes predominantly in the historical fiction, Christian fiction, comedy and romance genres.

Apart from writing fictional books, Brenda writes for her blogs blackhair101.com; where she gives hair care tips and fiwibooks.com, where she shares about her writing life.

You can connect with Brenda online at:
Brenda-Barrett.com
Twitter.com/AuthorWriterBB
Facebook.com/AuthorBrendaBarrett

Chapter One

Brandon let himself into his sister's self-contained basement flat and promptly sneezed. He switched on the light and looked around. There was a tiny hall space with a table jammed in the corner and a kitchenette with its counter covered with boxes of stuff.

He leaned on the door with a sigh and sneezed again. From where he stood he could see the double bed; it was covered with a white sheet and more boxes. His sister had confessed that this was where she had begun to store her junk since the garage was overflowing with too many of their odds and ends.

He pushed a box farther down on the counter area and rested his bag beside it.

The box cover had a bow on it, and when he looked closely he saw that it was a four-piece glass set that he and Ashley had given his sister and brother-in-law as an anniversary present three years ago. The red string still had the card attached to it and he opened it up, stalling for time. It read: *To Latoya and Richard, from Ashley and Brandon. Wishing you many more years together. Love you guys.*

He remembered when Ashley had chosen the present. He hadn't liked it at the time but he didn't dare say so because they had been quarreling more than ever that year and she had been pregnant with Ariel.

He had chosen the path of least resistance and had allowed her to do whatever she thought best because he had gotten tired of the constant battle. This present had just been a small representation of how far he had gone to avoid conflict. He would never have chosen glasses; he knew his sister's taste better than that. He could have predicted that this was where the gift would end up.

He closed his eyes tightly and then opened them again. Today had been the day that finally showed him that he should leave his home; he had to give up the fight. He had to preserve his sanity. If he hadn't left just now he would probably have been jailed for murder or hospitalized for a heart condition. He slumped on the counter; he didn't even want to think about what he had just seen.

He walked to the bed and sat on it; a plume of dust surrounded him. He jumped up, fanning the air, and then looked at his black pants; they had remnants of cobweb sticking to them. While he was busy dusting himself off a black shape darted from one side of a box and under another. It was a roach, and it was joined by an even bigger roach that didn't bother to hide but was looking at him curiously. The little critter seemed to be saying to him, 'shove off and find your own place.'

If it were another time Brandon would have found it funny but tonight his sense of humor was killed, maybe forever. He looked at the insect balefully and decided that he couldn't sleep here, not with them crawling around. He did not have the energy to clean the place and battle with roaches and who knows what else.

If Latoya and Richard didn't have a full house he would be at the main house now, but as it was, Latoya had taken one look at his face when he showed up at her door a few moments ago and given him a big sisterly hug.

"You have finally come to your senses and left that woman. I am so happy for you. Listen, I have a full house now," she whispered. "Richie's parents and their friends came in from England this evening. We are full to the hilt. You can use the flat. It is not altogether livable but it's just for the night. We can clean it up tomorrow."

He was happy that she hadn't pressed him for more because he wasn't sure that he wanted to tell anyone about what finally drove him from his marital home. Not even the counselor that he had insisted that he and Ashley see, for close to a year now, would he tell.

He had been fighting for his marriage for so long and so hard that he had not seen what was right under his nose. He grabbed his bag and headed out from the flat. He would go to a hotel, but his credit card was almost maxed out this month because Ashley had been redecorating her store. He took a deep breath.

Maybe he could try a guesthouse instead of a hotel; they were more reasonably priced. He headed for his car and got in, realizing when he started the car that the needle was on E.

He had nowhere to stay and as if all the forces of evil were against him, he had an empty gas tank to compound matters. At least the car started, and he drove off toward the gate. He fervently prayed that it wouldn't stop before he reached the gas station at the top of the road near Papine.

At least he had enough money to take care of gas. He

mentally counted the cash in his wallet; he could buy a bottled water and maybe a pack of biscuits. He realized how famished he was feeling all of a sudden. After the emotional bomb that was dropped on his head just a short while ago, his body was just processing practical physical feelings like hunger.

He drew up at the gas station and waited in line to get gas. It was barely nine o'clock. He took a mental inventory of the places around and tried to remember if he had seen a guesthouse in the area.

The knock on his window jolted him from his contemplation and he looked to see who it was. It was a girl, a very lovely girl. She was frantically indicating to him to wind down his window. He did so reluctantly. Something told him that this was not going to be good; it fitted in with his theme for the night.

"May I help you, miss?"

"Yes," she said breathlessly. "Could you let me in? I need to escape. I need to leave here," she said in a rush. "Can you help me?"

His eyes widened in consternation and he looked around. There was only the car before his. It was finally finished with the pump and was driving off.

The gas station attendant waved him up; he looked sleepy and unperturbed by this girl knocking on his window.

He looked across at the gas station mart; it was empty except for a lady who had a baby in her hand and was choosing snacks. The cashier was on the phone.

Life was going on placidly except for this girl who was skimpily dressed pleading with him to let her into his car.

Was this some kind of hoax?

She ran her hands through her long, thick, wavy hair and looked around wildly. He observed her in awe. She looked like someone who would not be out of place in a beauty pageant.

Was she some kind of prostitute, or was she a drag queen? He had been hearing stories about them lately—transvestites who were fooling men into thinking that they were women—but somehow she didn't look like she was in drag. Her pure features were showing a young woman in distress.

She opened her fingers in a gesture of supplication and mouthed, "Please."

He released the central lock and watched as she jumped in. Her perfume was overpowering, as if she took a bath in it.

She gave him a grateful look. "Thank you sir." She then dipped down in the seat. "He is out there. He doesn't know that I cut across the gas station. I had to run away; I really don't want him to find me. It was getting too much. I just want to go home."

Brandon observed her fully. Her hands were trembling as she clutched her silver purse. Her whole body was trembling like a newborn puppy.

"How old are you?" he asked, because close up, beyond the thickly applied mascara and foundation he could discern that she was not that old—probably younger than some of the freshmen at the university where he worked. That would make her a high schooler. He waited for her answer, which was given after a long hesitation.

"Fifteen," she muttered. "A mature fifteen," she added for good measure.

Fifteen and out at this time of night dressed like a prostitute and running away from a man.

He sighed. This was too much. He should not have gotten involved in this, whatever this was.

He drove up to the gas pump and drummed his finger on the steering wheel while the gas station attendant put the hose in the gas tank.

"So, what's your name?" he asked his young passenger, who looked as if she had slumped even further into the seat.

"Tara," she said weakly and then her voice hitched as if she was sobbing. "Could you take me home to my sister?"

"Where does your sister live?" Brandon asked. He paid the attendant and drove onto the main road. He couldn't stop for the biscuit and water he wanted to get at the gas station mart; he had to think of his stowaway.

He didn't want whomever Tara was escaping from to find her. She looked genuinely disturbed and besides, she was a minor. Maybe he should let the police handle it. Her family was probably looking for her anyway.

"My sister lives in Forest Hills."

The other side of town...great, Brandon thought, turning the car in that direction.

When he approached Waterloo road Tara sat up in the seat.

"Thank you so much. I am sorry about all of this."

"You were running away from a man and you ran into a stranger's car without knowing if I am dangerous or not." Brandon's raised his brows at her. "You are extremely trusting in this day and age."

"You don't look dangerous," Tara said flippantly. "You are in a suit and tie and you drive a nice late model car; you have a baby seat in the back and you have kind eyes. I thought about that before I knocked on the window."

"Kind-eyed strangers with baby seats in the back of their cars have been known to do very bad things to women."

"But you wouldn't need to do bad things to women," Tara grinned. "You are extremely good-looking. I am sure women are the ones who want to do bad things to you." She laughed and slapped her leg.

The scared teenager who had stopped his car a few

moments ago was gone. She had recovered quickly, but the mascara tracks on her cheeks were telling him another story.

"What are you doing out at night dressed like that?" Brandon asked.

"I ran away from home a couple days ago." Tara closed her eyes. "I was staying with my boyfriend but as it turns out, he is a real pig."

"Your boyfriend?" Brandon asked incredulously. "Did he run away from home too?"

"My boyfriend is an older guy," Tara said. "He has his own home and a few other women that I am just finding out about."

Brandon resisted a loud sigh; he knew all could not be well with her home life. Children who had a stable family environment did not just run away from home like this. That made him think about his own family life. He had two girls, one seven and one three years old. His home life was looking bleak right now, maybe broken beyond repair. Would this be the way that his oldest, Alisha, would be in a couple of years, or even his youngest, innocent Ariel?

They wouldn't understand why Daddy wasn't coming home anymore and God knows what sort of lifestyle they would end up living with their mother as a role model.

He cursed Ashley in his head and then gritted his teeth. Through the years he had tried to hold it together for them. No matter how absolutely wretched things had gotten with Ashley, he had tried to hold their relationship together.

But tonight...tonight... Ashley had just taken it a step too far, and he could not in all good conscience deal with their marriage, not for a second more—not even for his babies. It made no sense when only one person was trying to piece together a broken relationship. No sense at all...

He tore his mind away from the scene in his head and

forcefully dragged it back to the present and to Tara, who was looking through the passenger window forlornly.

"You said I should drop you at your sister's place? Where are your parents?"

"They are divorced," Tara said, "and they each have their own families. I am the odd one out for all of them. My mom," her voice cracked, "has a new baby, a boy. The much longed-for boy. She doesn't care about me. I doubt if they even miss me, and my dad is closer to his stepdaughters than he is to me, his own flesh and blood. Only Nadine will probably care that I am missing."

"Nadine is your sister?" Brandon asked.

"Yes," Tara murmured, "my older sister. She was spared the kind of childhood I had because she is older by ten years. Do you have kids?" she asked him, apparently tired of talking about herself.

"Yes, two very sweet girls," Brandon said. "They are my life."

"Aww." Tara sighed, "There was a time when my parents had just two girls and they lived together and we were a regular family. Now we have all sorts of strangers butting into our lives on both sides of the family tree. It is pathetic."

Brandon grimaced. "It happens."

"No," Tara scowled, "it doesn't just happen. People give up on their commitment to each other and they find other people who are more attractive to have sex with. First it was my dad. He did the cliché and had an affair with his next-door neighbor, and then my mom followed and had an affair with her business partner. And then both of them decided that they would amicably divorce because they were no longer compatible with each other. Divorce and amicable should never go together. Never. Nobody thought about me." She sniffed and then muttered under her breath, "I don't even know your name."

"Brandon Blake." Brandon flashed her a smile. "That's okay. I understand the need to vent."

"You happily married, Brandon?" Tara whispered.

"Not happily." Brandon glanced at her. "Sorry to add to the doom and gloom."

"It's okay," Tara said, "tonight is a night for it."

Exactly what he had thought earlier. Brandon nodded, agreeing with her.

He drove up to Forest Hills, an affluent neighborhood. He slowed down the car when Tara indicated a gate. "It's right here."

It was a large house, on a substantial lot. He could see that all the lights were on, even the lights on the gate. He blew the horn and the door at the top flew open and then a lady came outside on the balcony in jeans and a white sweater. She was on the phone.

"That's her," Tara said excitement in her voice. "That's Nadine."

And then another lady joined her on the veranda with a baby.

"That's my mom; what is she doing here?"

And yet another came on the veranda. "That's my stepmother," Tara groaned. "I can't believe she is here too."

Brandon chuckled. "So much for your theory that nobody cares, huh?"

Tara got out of the car and waved, and all the ladies shared a sigh of collective relief. Even from where he sat in the car, Brandon could see the happiness on their faces. He had in essence brought home the prodigal daughter.

The girl in white sweater was the first to come down the stairs. The gate swung open at the same time and Brandon contemplated just turning around and driving away but he figured he should give some sort of explanation so he drove through, with Tara walking slowly beside the car, her back hunched over.

"This is my sister, Nadine," Tara said to him when he stepped out of the car and onto the cobblestone driveway. "Nadine this is Brandon, who rescued me tonight."

Nadine was busy hugging her and whispering, "Thank God you are home."

Brandon nodded. She was still in the shadows but when she came into the light fully, he recognized her. He struggled not to be impressed when he saw that this Nadine was actually Nadine Langley, the singer and producer.

One day he saw her picture on the cover of *Caribbean Beat* magazine, and he studied her smiling face for a full five minutes and wondered if she was as sweet and innocent as she looked, or if she was nasty, cantankerous, and rude.

It must have been when he was at a low point and was feeling cynical, probably after an argument with Ashley, and he had been trying to disassociate himself from his problems.

He had to admit that Nadine was just as pretty in real life, without a ton of makeup or Photoshop—even better than her magazine pictures. Her eyes had a natural cat-like curve and her bare lips were pink and plump. She wore her hair in a short pageboy style.

She looked a lot younger in person. It was easy to forget that she was a young person because of her production track record. She produced for some big-name artists and had recently released a single that was doing well internationally.

In the magazine article she was dubbed as the young musical genius who was about to take over the world, which wasn't hard for her to do; she belonged to a royal family of musicians. Her grandfather, Gramps Langley, was still a sought-after artiste and her grandmother, Siddany Langley, was an actress and singer.

"Hi." She held out her hand and pumped his. "Thank you for bringing Tara home."

"I was actually quite pleased to do so," Brandon said, feeling her soft hand in his and holding it for a fraction too long. "It is a dangerous place out there, especially for a girl her age, and she seemed frantic when she knocked on my window at the gas station."

"Come on in and join us. I am sure the whole family would like to thank you."

"No, sorry." Brandon shook his head. "It was nice meeting you and I am happy that I brought the prodigal home. I am sure she is quite capable of telling her story without me being present." He turned to his car. "I have to find somewhere to stay tonight. It is getting late."

"Bye Brandon," Tara said, waving as her mother and stepmother surrounded her and herded her inside.

"Bye Tara. Be good." He looked around again. Nadine was still standing there with a bemused look on her face.

"You were going to stay at a hotel tonight?" she asked.

"Well," Brandon leaned on the car door, "not quite. I was thinking of a guest house or something."

"Why?" Nadine came closer to him. "Aren't you from around here?"

He could smell her perfume, a subtle sweet scent that made him feel nostalgic, like he had smelled that scent sometime before, in a different time, when life was better, when he was happier. Her hazel eyes were alive with curiosity.

He felt like shocking her and telling her that of course he was from around here. He was a professor at the university of technology, heading the engineering department. He was just a man without a place to stay. His wife had done the unthinkable and he just needed a chance to unwind and sleep tonight before he could process what on earth he was going to do next.

When he found himself saying just that, he watched as her eyes widened in shock. He sighed and got in the car. "Well, goodnight then."

"Wait," she said. "I have a furnished apartment, in Smoky Vale. It's not far from here. I usually reserve it for visiting artistes. It is close to the studio in a private and secure gated complex. It has a lovely view of the city and nobody is staying there now."

"You don't know me," Brandon said softly, looking into her concerned eyes.

"You are the guy that brought my sister back to us," Nadine said, "and it seems as if you need a place to crash...one is available. Wait here, I'll get the key."

Brandon relaxed in the seat and closed his eyes. He was feeling somewhat bemused. He hadn't counted on the fact that his one Good Samaritan deed would result in him getting a place to stay tonight.

She came back to the window and handed him the key. "It's apartment number three, Smoky Vale Terrace."

"Thanks, I'll bring this back tomorrow," he said, jingling the key. Suddenly he felt bone tired, like too many things had gone on and he needed to blank out.

"No worries," Nadine said, nodding. "Here's my card; you can call me."

He took the card and drove off, leaving her standing in the middle of the driveway staring after him.

Chapter Two

Nadine turned to go back into the house long after the car had reversed out of the yard. Tara was standing at the door with a cross look on her face.

"They are arguing about me and where I am supposed to live. Dad is the loudest one, as usual. Even the stepfather is here. What are they doing here, anyway?"

Nadine looked at her sister and frowned. "Can you imagine they actually care about you? They descended upon the house, all thinking that you had disappeared. Mom thought you had gone to Dad, as you sometimes do to freak her out, and Dad thought you had gone to Mom. Where were you for three days, T?"

"With Trey, but we were at a party at Roy's house and then Trey's girlfriend came over with her kid and then a fight started."

"A fight?" Nadine shuddered. "You weren't hurt?" She didn't even bother to ask who Trey was, or any of the other persons that Tara mentioned. Tara changed boyfriends regularly and short of locking her up in a mini-prison somewhere, the family was pretty much resigned to the fact that she was going to do what she wanted to do.

"The fight wasn't between me and Trey at first. It was with him and his skank girlfriend. I said I was leaving and then Trey threatened me and tried to hold me down and then I ran out of the place and..." she sighed. "It was ugly…shouting and screaming and then he pulled out his gun and... It was a good thing I met Brandon at the gas station. I just got out of there."

Nadine shuddered when she heard the patchy account of Tara's fight. "This Trey person had a gun?"

"Yep," Tara said. "It is legal, though. He is a security guard."

"Yeah, right." Nadine sighed. Her sister's life was more drama filled at fifteen than hers was at twenty-five.

"Daddy said he is going to get Trey locked up for statutory rape. He said he is going hunt him down, as if I am going to tell them who Trey really is. Trey didn't even know that I was fifteen, and he doesn't know that I am a Langley. I wish they would all go away. Mom, Dad, the witch!"

"Heather is not a witch," Nadine scolded. "She was the first one to tell me that you were missing. She was frantic with worry. She came here tonight and gathered the troops together. We had just gotten off the phone with a detective friend of Dad's when you showed up."

"It figures that it was the witch who was concerned about me, and she's just a stepmother," Tara sighed dramatically. "My real parents didn't even miss me for three whole days. I am just a waste of space."

Nadine stood in front of her sister and tried to work out what to say. As her big sister she had tried to counsel Tara in the past. Their parents had gone to counseling with her but Tara was determined to punish them for turning her world topsy-turvy. She wanted them to hurt for finding other partners, and she was succeeding.

Nadine felt impotent in the face of all of this teenage angst and rebellion. She and Tara were chalk and cheese, maybe because they had vastly different childhoods.

She had spent most of her time with her grandparents on both sides of the family. With Gramps Langley she had learned how to play several musical instruments and create sounds. She had literally grown up learning how to produce music. It had been a joy to spend so much time in the studio. That had been her life; she had not gotten the chance to be a rebellious teenager.

On the other hand, Tara had no such outlet. She found the whole musical side of things boring. Instead, she was fixated on the fact that her life had changed for the worse.

Tara had taken the divorce hard. She had just been ten, the center of their parents' universe, and then it all changed.

"We have come to a conclusion," her father said behind Tara. "We are sending you to your grandparents in the country. When they are finished with you, I'll see if you will continue to be such a brat. Something has to be done before you end up on drugs, or worse."

"Oh Lord, not that," Tara rolled her eyes. "They don't even have Internet in their poky little country house, and they don't have cable television. Daddy, please, no!"

"It will do you good," Will Langley said gruffly. "Tara, you are just fifteen, and you went missing for three days. Do you know how that makes me feel?"

Tara snorted unrepentantly. "It should make you feel like you want your original family back."

Her father grunted. "It's not going to happen, Tara. Accept

it."

"Never," Tara hissed. " I am not related to your wife or Mommy's husband and new baby. I hate them all and if you send me to the grandparents' I'll just run away again."

Her father gave her an exasperated look. "Where would you run to? They live in a remote area of the Blue Mountains. You'll love it; you can help out at the Inn they operate there."

"No!" Tara turned to Nadine. "Nads, don't let them make me."

Nadine looked at her father, who had a determined expression on his face. She thought it was a brilliant idea. Away from the city and all the distractions, maybe Tara would learn some old-fashioned values.

She had stayed with her mother's parents in the Blue Mountains every summer until she was eighteen, and it had been rustic and fun. Her grandparents were strict, God-fearing people who subscribed to simplicity and good living, and there was always something to do and new people to meet when hikers stopped by overnight on their way to Blue Mountain Peak.

She then looked at Tara's pleading expression and shook her head. "Sorry Tara. I am actually siding with them this time."

Tara's face crumpled. "I can't believe you hate me too. I should have just spent the night with Brandon."

Will Langley threw his hands up in the air and turned to go back inside. "This girl, this girl, I don't know...get ready to leave in five minutes, Tara. We should get out of Nadine's hair; she needs her sleep. You are coming home with me."

"You'll be fine." Nadine patted Tara on her unyielding back.

"Thanks for nothing," Tara growled. "All of you make me sick."

She stormed back inside and then spun around. "Don't you go catching feelings for Brandon; he's married. I saw the way you were looking at him just now!"

Nadine chuckled dryly. "He was not that visible in the semi-dark."

"Yes, he was," Tara insisted. "He's really good looking and you spent a long time looking after him when his car went down the driveway."

"I don't think your judgment holds any credibility right now," Nadine said without heat. "I will never date a married man, no matter how fine he is."

She completely ignored the part of her that was eagerly waiting to see him tomorrow when he returned the key to the apartment.

Chapter Three

Ashley Blake sat in the spacious living room in a silk robe, a cup of tea in her hand. Her friend Regina sat before her.

"You should just divorce Brandon now. Cut off all ties; get full custody of the kids. Take the house. Do it before he does. I saw him tonight; he looked as if he was a man who could cause serious problems for you."

"No!" Ashley stood up and looked outside at the walkway. "This is all your fault, Regina."

"My fault? Really? Your time with Brandon ran its course a long time ago. Divorce him before he divorces you," Regina urged

Ashley felt like yelling for Regina to stop and get out but she kept her voice even. She learned a long time ago that Regina had to be handled with care; she could be dangerous and she knew too many secrets.

Ashley kept her tone even and turned to Regina. "I mean, I could divorce him now and he wouldn't put up a fight, but he will fight for custody of the kids. He loves them."

"That's your bargaining tool, then," Regina said. "Make him pay. You have something that he wants, and don't go all soft on him; Brandon is from a wealthy family. Isn't that why you married him in the first place and did that elaborate church-sister-thingy?"

"No!" Ashley yelped. "I love Brandon. That's why I married him. Love. Nothing else. I have always felt so unworthy of him in a way because of my background and... you know."

Regina snorted. "No, I don't."

"Brandon is so nice. He's caring and loyal and he's a family man. I feel so bad about him finding out..."

"Oh, shut up already about him finding out. I told him about that before you guys got married and he still got married to you. He wanted to marry you so much eight years ago that he ignored everything. Too bad for him. Nice guys finish last." Regina grinned wickedly. "Kick him to the curb. It is high time."

"I have to play this very carefully," Ashley moved away from the curtains and looked at Regina fully. "I can't just kick him to the curb as callously as you are suggesting. The boutique is finally in the black and we are doing quite well, but Brandon has always filled in if there is a shortfall, and he takes care of the house—and private school fees for the kids are not cheap. Besides, I feel very bad about this whole thing tonight."

Ashley sank into the armchair closest to her. She carefully placed the cup of tea on the side table and looked up at Regina, who was looking at her expectantly.

"You have to go, Regina. I need some time alone."

"No, Ashley," Regina said forcefully. "I am here with you through thick and thin. I got your back."

"I know that you have my back," Ashley said tiredly. "I am not sure what I want to do just yet. Maybe I still have a chance with Brandon. I could call him, beg his forgiveness."

"No." Regina crouched down beside Ashley's chair. "I am all you need."

Ashley frowned. She hated when Regina got all possessive and needy. She was feeling a little revulsion about what happened earlier and for getting caught. She didn't want Regina around while she struggled to come to terms with the look of fiery condemnation that she had seen in Brandon's eyes, the look that said it was over.

He hadn't articulated it but she had felt it and it was making her feel afraid, repentant and slightly nauseous.

Her conscience, which she had thought was dormant, was well and truly awakened, making her feel like the lowest of the low. She felt exactly like the time when her dad had caught her stealing when she was in first grade. Back then she had wanted the floor to open up and swallow her alive. She was kind of feeling that way now, hours after Brandon had left the house.

She did not want to break up her family, at least not now. Though she had always thought that leaving Brandon would be a breeze, and to be honest she had considered doing just that at various times over the years, she had not prepared herself for him to do it first.

The first six months after their marriage, she seriously considered just leaving him and calling it a day. Carlos King, her colleague at the bank where she had worked, had inspired some wayward thoughts in her and she had tried to resist him, but seven months to the day after she said "I do" to Brandon she and Carlos had indulged in a very torrid affair. Carlos had made her feel normal. She could be herself with him, and not as if she was playing a role, which she felt she was doing 99% of the time with Brandon.

She had contemplated leaving Brandon then but she had stayed when Alisha was born and the affair with Carlos fizzled out. A pregnant married woman was not all that attractive to him.

Since then her rocky relationship with Brandon had seen many ups and downs. Mostly downs. To be honest, she was not the typical wife, at least not the kind of wife that Brandon wanted, and one day she just got tired of pretending.

She knew that Brandon wanted a woman that was patterned after his mother, the paragon of virtue, Beatrice Blake.

She hated the fact that she was not the best wife she could be; she liked to be the best at everything. She liked to win and her marriage pointed out to her every day that she had failed. Right now, she did not expect this feeling of guilt, which seemed to be humming along her nerves. It was telling her that she had gambled with her marriage and lost.

Regina clutched her hand and her nails dug into her wrist. Ashley shook her off and got up.

"It's late. Alisha has a field trip tomorrow and I have to pick her up from her grandmother's and take her to school earlier than usual."

"I can sleep over." Regina gave her a meaningful look. "It's not as if Brandon will be here glowering about my presence and there are no kids—just you and me, like old times."

"No, just go." Ashley went toward the front door.

"Can I come over tomorrow?" Regina asked, walking behind Ashley with no haste in her steps.

Ashley opened the door and waited for an eternity while Regina stopped and looked at her contemplatively.

"I'll call you," Ashley said, knowing she wouldn't. She had reached almost the end of her tether with Regina. If Regina hadn't come over earlier threatening to expose her latest secret she wouldn't be in this predicament now.

She slumped on the door weakly when Regina finally left. She was in deep trouble. She may have used up all her chances with Brandon.

Chapter Four

Brandon let himself into the two-bedroom apartment at Smoky Vale Terrace and breathed a sigh of relief. The place was a far cry from the dusty accommodations at his sister's. It was spacious and simply furnished. It had black leather settees in the living room, a glass center table, and a black and white zebra rug.

The black and white theme continued into the bedrooms, and he chose the bigger one with the king-sized bed.

Before he threw himself down into the inviting bed, he opened the windows around the apartment to let in fresh air. It was chilly outside, especially since it had rained earlier and it was nearing December.

He then headed to the shower and looked at himself in the mirror. He hadn't changed physically, he reassured himself; he hadn't grown a streak of white hair from excessive stress. For a moment tonight he had thought that he very well could have.

He headed into the shower and closed his eyes under the driving water and tried to keep the recall at bay. The incident with Tara had distracted him somewhat and had turned out to be a blessing. At least he had a place to stay tonight but that had proven to be a small respite; it just helped him to sweep the rage aside for a while.

Now he felt his heart rate gathering speed as the day appeared in his mind's eye. He had woken up at six o'clock as usual, and he had gone to the children's room. Alisha had kicked off the covers and was curled up in a ball, her hands under her chin in a pose of supplication. He hated to wake her up when she looked that peaceful but he had to if they were going to beat the traffic and get to school on time.

He shook her awake and watched as her eyelids slowly fluttered and she opened her eyes sleepily.

"Come on, honey," he had whispered to her, "time to get going."

He always stood and watched that she didn't go back to sleep. When he was satisfied that she was functionally awake, he went over to Ariel's bed.

Ariel was a little harder to get out of bed but he managed it eventually, carrying her to the shower and giving her a quick warm bath and then getting her dressed.

He put her in the playpen in the living room and went to have his own shower. He did this as stealthily as he could because Ashley did not enjoy being woken up before seven.

She had no idea what their routine was in the morning. He was the one who concerned himself about what to get them for breakfast. He was the one who fielded the questions and listened to the comments about school.

This morning was the usual chitchat and banter with him and the girls. Ashley came down the stairs sleepily.

"Morning family," she said to them generally and headed

for the teapot.

"Mommy, I have a field trip to the art museum tomorrow," Alisha said, talking with her mouth almost full of scrambled eggs.

"Good," Ashley said. "In my days at prep school we never had stuff like that."

Brandon resisted the urge to roll his eyes at Ashley. She never went to prep school. Ashley had grown up rough in the ghetto and had gone to a government school near where she lived. These days she was creating a fantasy past in order to impress the people around her. He had spoken to her about it but that discussion ended up in an argument.

"Miss Jackson said that we can even paint our own pictures," Alisha said. "I am really looking forward to it."

"Who is Miss Jackson again?" Ashley looked at him curiously.

Brandon raised his eyebrow. "Her new teacher, the one who replaced Miss Eldermire."

"Oh," Ashley said and yawned. "I just can't keep up with the attrition rate at your prep school, Alisha. It's appalling."

Alisha looked at her mother, confused, and then turned to him.

"Daddy, what's attrition?" Alisha asked him after Ashley's comment. That was another irritating habit that Ashley had picked up; talking above the children's level. Brandon sighed and explained attrition and then appalling while he cleaned off the front of Ariel's dress.

Ashley stood sipping her tea and looking at them as if she was not a part of the family. He hated that. It was as if she gave birth to them and then handed them over to him. He did not feel as if he was co-parenting or part of a cohesive unit.

He had the full responsibility for his girls and their mother was right there like a bystander. He had given in and hired a sitter a year after Ariel was born. He could not play Mr. Mom, juggle his busy job as head of a university engineering department, and work on lucrative private contracts at the same time.

Ariel did not share much of a bond with her mother because of Ashley's hands-off approach to parenting, and Brandon was beginning to get worried. When he mentioned it to Ashley they argued, so he was choosing the time carefully to mention it again.

"Ariel has an appointment with the dentist today," he reminded Ashley. It was on the calendar taped on the notice board above the breakfast nook and circled in bright red, but of course he had to remind Ashley or else Ariel would not be taken to the dentist.

"Oh," Ashley looked at him and then shrugged, "let Juliet take her."

"Today is Juliet's day off." He felt himself getting irritated, as he so often did these days when Ashley spoke.

"Then have your mom take her. She was complaining the other day that she doesn't see them as often as she should. Maybe she can take them for the night too."

Brandon sighed. "Okay, whatever. Arrange it with her."

He made it very clear from his tone that he was not going to do the arranging too. He picked up Ariel. "Let's get you cleaned up. Come on, Alisha, you too."

When he came back from the bathroom Ashley was still standing at the counter staring through the window at the pool, a faraway look in her eyes.

"I'll be home late," he said abruptly.

"Okay." She swung her head around, and a few tendrils of her hair caught in her eyes. She pulled it back, gave him one of those smiles that didn't quite reach her eyes and then tucked her hair behind her ears.

"Bye Mommy," Alisha called from the door.

Ashley waved and smiled.

Ariel didn't turn back for a kiss or tell her bye and Ashley didn't force it.

She cheerfully said, "Bye guys" and continued staring out the window in that apathetic way of hers that was grinding on Brandon's last nerve.

He felt as if he was going to blow a blood vessel just thinking about how cold and distant she was from her own children.

Ariel put her hand trustingly in his and looked up at him, a grin on her face.

He felt his blood pressure decreasing and he smiled at his daughter. She looked nothing like him or Ashley; she was light, almost biracial, with golden hair and eyes. His parents joked that Ariel must have reached back far into the gene pool and gotten something from some unknown ancestor.

He strapped her into the car seat and watched as Alisha sat in the car, her expression serious. She was the quiet, introspective child who loved to read and to learn 'big' words; in that regard her mother was surely helping her out, he conceded grudgingly.

He smiled at her warmly and made sure that her seat belt was fastened. She didn't look like either him or Ashley either; she was as dark as Ariel was light, with the sweetest little heart-shaped face. She had a pale yellow birthmark on her cheek shaped like a heart. She was going to be an extremely beautiful girl when she grew up--and bright too.

Already she was smarter than the children her own age. They were sending her to classes for gifted children. Her teachers were contemplating placing her two grade levels above where she was now.

After dropping Ariel at pre-school and Alisha at prep

school he headed to work, listening to the local news station.

He had a smooth day at the office pushing papers and putting out a potential fire or two. Being head of the department was becoming predictable; even the occasional department crisis was becoming routine. So when his friend, Harold Mercer, called near the end of the day and for the umpteenth time begged him to relocate to Canada to come and work with him in his engineering firm, he was more than amenable to the idea.

"We need civil engineers, man. Relocate the family and come up."

Brandon had found himself seriously toying with the idea while Harold gave his usual sales pitch.

The truth was his family could do with the change; maybe it would be the answer to saving his marriage.

He hesitated in answering for the first time since Harold had started badgering him to relocate. And as if Harold sensed his hesitancy he pressed, "Just come up for three months in the New Year, and see if you like it."

"I'll think about it," Brandon had told Harold coolly, not wanting to encourage his friend and end up disappointing him in the long run.

He could mention it to Ashley and see if she would be willing to relocate. His contract as head of the engineering department was a temporary one and would be up in six weeks. The university was making noises about offering him a permanent contract but he wasn't so sure he wanted that. Paper pushing was never his thing; he liked to be out in the field. Big projects excited him; building roads, highways and stadiums was his main joy.

He had gone home in a good mood. Maybe this evening, with no kids at home, he could have a heart-to-heart with Ashley. They had not had any meaningful conversation for months, if not years; they could discuss what was next for them.

He was chafing at the superficiality of their relationship. They had descended into politeness, sometimes going so far as discussing the weather like strangers at a bus stop. Ironically, they hadn't even discussed the weather in weeks, but he wanted more from his marriage. It was beginning to feel like he was in prison, and Ashley was growing more and more distant and non-communicative. It was as if he was living with a hostile cell mate and he was clueless as to why.

He drove up in the tree-lined driveway and parked behind a Honda Integra with a grinning skeleton on the side. He sighed. The car was a bright yellow, which meant that Ashley had company in the form of Regina, her tattooed and multi-pierced friend from high school. Regina rubbed him the wrong way, with her brash attitude and flippant way of speaking.

He hated Regina. It was something he was praying about. He shouldn't hate people but usually the thought of Regina was enough to make him angry. He didn't want her around his children and he definitely didn't want her around his wife. She was brash and rude and swore indiscriminately when he was around. He was sure that she did it because she wanted to make him mad.

In his estimation, Regina was responsible for fifty percent of their marital problems. Whenever she came around she was like a black cloud that announced a coming storm. Her presence was usually enough for Ashley to change into an aloof person with him. He could usually tell if Ashley spoke to Regina or had seen her the day before; she snapped and snarled at him and everyone around her after seeing her.

Last year he and Ashley had had the mother of all showdowns when she had gotten a butterfly tattoo on her lower back, matching one that Regina had. It had irked him that Ashley was still so impressionable and acted like a vapid teenager when Regina was around, quite unlike the adult that she usually claimed that she was.

He had a dark scowl on his face when he let himself into the house. It only got darker when he heard giggling coming from upstairs.

He marched upstairs and pushed open the master bedroom door, which was slightly ajar; he was going to yell. He didn't want Regina in his bedroom. He was going to tell her to get out of his house and make it permanent. He didn't care if Ashley found his draconian measures offensive.

He pushed the slightly ajar door and realized two things at the same time. One: his wife was naked and on top of Regina. Both of them were giggling and thrashing around on the bed in the throes of passion.

And two: he was an idiot. A first class idiot who should have seen that there was more to their friendship than them being mere 'besties' who hung out together. All the signs had been there through the years.

Regina dressed and acted like a man. Regina being possessive over Ashley to the point of discomfort. Regina telling him on the eve of his wedding that he would have to share Ashley with her.

He had stood at the door for the longest time, a ringing in his ear. His voice had fled and there was a haze surrounding his vision.

When Ashley had sensed that they were no longer alone and had looked over at him, he could not speak. He imagined that he must have looked like a kicked dog. He wasn't even mad. He was disappointed, a bone-deep disappointment that had rooted him to the floor.

He registered that Ashley had jumped up from her friend's

naked body and wrapped herself in a robe and that Regina had had the gall to sneer at him, lying on her side, her small breasts still glistening with Ashley's spittle. She laughed at him.

"Hi Brandon, you should have announced that you were home. We could have finished up before."

"Shut up, Regina," Ashley hissed. "Brandon, listen, I can explain." She yanked up a robe that was discarded at the foot of the bed and covered her bare breasts. Her brown eyes were glittering with fearful anxiety. "Please...this isn't what you think..."

"It isn't?" Brandon could not recall ever making so much effort to speak. His initial shock was melting into rage and a sickening sense of disbelief.

"We were just playing around...." Ashley urged in the charged silence. She moved closer and made a pleading movement with her hands.

Regina snorted from the bed. She was still lying there with a pleased curve to her lips, as if she was relishing the drama that was taking place around her.

"How often do you do this?" Brandon gritted, his pulse beating like a drum. He didn't even know if he was asking the right questions. "Do you do this with the kids in the house?"

"No!" Ashley squeaked. "It's not as if Regina is a guy or anything, so technically it's not cheating." She reached out for his hand. "It's nothing for you to worry about or even think about. I swear it won't ever happen again, and I've never done this with the kids in the house."

Brandon backed out of her reach. His mind couldn't grasp the fact that his wife of eight years was telling him that catching her in bed with another person wasn't cheating.

He felt betrayed. He felt incredulous. He was almost

speechless with the thousand and one high volts of emotions rocking through him.

"I understand that you are shocked and furious but I am sorry," Ashley said in a panicked rush.

He was not responding and she was wringing her hands guiltily. "I'll make it up to you, I swear."

"How will you make it up to me?" Brandon asked, a sneer in his voice. "Join the two of you in bed and pretend that this never happened?"

"You would do that?" Ashley asked, relieved. "That would be great wouldn't it, Regina?" She turned to her friend who was still lounging in bed and watching them with a bored expression on her face.

"I don't think that was a serious offer," Regina said, sensing that Brandon was about to explode.

A shudder of angry revulsion passed through Brandon. Ashley's stupidity in assuming that his question was a bid to join her in her immoral ménage a trois made him realize that he didn't even know this woman. He was married to her for eight years and he just realized that he was living with and trying to make a marriage work with a stranger.

"I am leaving," Brandon breathed. "I can't deal with this right now. I may not be able to ever deal with this."

"You can't be serious!" Ashley gasped in stricken horror. "Just calm down and listen to reason, Brandon. Who is going to take care of Alisha and Ariel if you leave?"

"Maybe you should, for a change!" Brandon snorted. "But then again, I don't want you around my kids."

Brandon headed to his walk-in closet for a small travel bag. He realized that he hadn't unpacked from a business trip that he had taken two weeks before at an engineering symposium; he had just dumped the bag in the closet. He took it back up. It had everything that he would need for a week away from home. He would have to get some of the clothes cleaned, though.

"Brandon!" Ashley walked behind him, her shoulder length hair tousled from Regina's hands. Her lips bee-stung plump. Her big oval shaped eyes fearful. She was a beautiful woman, even with the stench of deception clinging to her.

He gave her a withering look of reproach that was pregnant with meaning; she had stopped trying to run behind him to explain the unexplainable, to beg him to stay—her lover stubbornly lounging in the marital bed like she belonged there.

He drove out of the yard without calling Ashley the names that were on the tip of his tongue. He turned off his phone when he saw that Ashley had called him several times. He could not bear to hear her voice, not tonight.

He stepped out of the shower, his blood still boiling as the scene replayed itself in his head. He dried himself off vigorously and rummaged in the bag for a pajama bottom, put it on and lay on the bed. He didn't expect to sleep but passed out from exhaustion.

*****

There were so many things a person had to consider in the aftermath of discovering that your wife was a cheating on you with a woman and had possibly been doing it for years.

Brandon headed to Nadine's house and ticked off the things that he needed to do in his head. All of them involved leaving Ashley for good, but he had the children to consider. Ashley wouldn't have the first clue about what to do with them. He would be punishing his girls if he stayed away. Ariel, especially, would have a tough time without him. He needed to think this through. Things would be chaotic for a few mornings. Maybe they wouldn't even show up at school, because Ashley was not one to rouse herself to wake up in time to take them. Juliet did not arrive for work until in the afternoons when she collected Ariel from pre-school, and then Alisha. She usually left late in the evenings after she prepared them for bed.

He drove up the hill to Nadine's place and turned into the yard when he saw that the gate was wide open. The place looked even more immaculate in the soft morning light. He admired her white Christmas plants, which wound all the way to the top of the driveway in fat, fluffy white blooms, reminiscent of snow. He stepped out of the car and onto a cobblestone driveway, and a ginger cat wound itself around his legs and greeted him with high-pitched meows.

He smiled down at the creature and resisted the urge to pet it; already his black pants had ginger cat hairs clinging to it where the cat was rubbing his head.

Nobody stirred in the house, and he reached into his pocket for the phone and took out Nadine's business card to call her when the front door opened and Nadine stood there smiling.

"Hi Brandon." She came down the steps hurriedly. "I was about to fix breakfast; want to join me?"

Brandon's stomach grumbled, reminding him that he hadn't eaten for close to twenty-four hours.

"Good morning, Nadine. Thank you so much for the use of your apartment. To be honest, I would really love to have breakfast. I am famished."

"Good, come on in then." She held the door opened and the cat joined them.

Nadine laughed, "Sorry, where're my manners? Brandon, meet Cat Langley."

Brandon chuckled. "I already met Cat."

"It figures. Cat loves men. I don't know why she adopted

me a couple of years ago." Nadine chuckled. "She rules this place with an iron paw."

"You live here alone?" he asked, looking around in the high-ceilinged hall and the spacious living room area. The decor was comfy and inviting. There were several black and white photos of famous musicians scattered throughout.

Nadine threw him an inscrutable look. "Yes, I live here alone—except for Cat, of course. It was three-bedroom fixer-upper when I bought it."

"I didn't mean to pry," Brandon stuttered. It had belatedly occurred to him that his question was probably intrusive.

Nadine headed to the kitchen and opened a glass door leading onto a patio. She turned to him. Her eyes had a twinkle in them, as if she found his apology amusing.

"It's a logical question to ask and since I don't believe that you are an axe murderer or anything, it's no problem to answer. I checked you out, by the way. You have a nice mug shot on the university's website."

"That's very wise of you to do, and thanks for the compliment," Brandon said, following behind her.

Nadine grinned. "What do you want for breakfast? I have a whole selection of breakfast foods. My helper, Lily, stocks up on breakfast stuff, like cereal, eggs...fixings for porridge—and she knows I hardly eat breakfast stuff for breakfast. I am more of a green juice kind of girl."

Brandon rolled up his sleeves. "I can make an omelet for us, and some toast and orange juice. That's simple enough."

Nadine turned surprised eyes on him. "Sure. Why not? I never refuse an offer from somebody else to take over the kitchen."

Especially an offer from a handsome man, she thought silently. She watched as he flashed her a grin. He was really good-looking in the light of day. He had the same facial profile as the actor Blair Underwood. His eyelashes were ridiculously long for a guy and when he smiled it was reflected in his eyes.

She sat at the counter and watched him as he moved around her kitchen as if he belonged there. He was efficient in the kitchen, as if he had fixed breakfast a hundred times before.

"Has anybody ever told you that you resemble Blair Underwood?" Nadine asked out loud.

Brandon looked at her and grinned. "Yes, countless times. Has anybody ever told you that you resemble Nadine Langley?"

"Ha," Nadine laughed. "I had a couple of interviews with magazines and a feature on entertainment television, a one-off hit song and suddenly I am famous."

"So modest. You and your family are famous," Brandon said. "I am kind of in awe that I am in your kitchen fixing breakfast."

"As you personally experienced last night," Nadine said regretfully, "my family has its share of problems. We are not exactly the best people to be in awe of."

"So what will become of Tara?" Brandon asked after finding the eggs and whipping them up in a bowl.

Nadine shook her head. "My parents decided to send her to my mom's parents in the country. They live in the Blue Mountains."

Brandon nodded. "That doesn't sound like a bad idea. They wanted to get her out of the Kingston environment, huh?"

"Yup." Nadine nodded. "Though I think she will protest against it for a while. I would love to have her here with me. We tried that last year but Tara started posing as an eighteen year old. She came down to the studio and was propositioning some of Grandpa's friends, so we sent her back to Dad's place and then Mom's, but when Mom got pregnant, she was sick for a while so she was sent back to Dad's."

"That's a terrible way for a child to live." Brandon sighed. "She's caught up in the middle; no wonder she is acting out."

"Do you have kids?" Nadine asked after a pause where Brandon seemed as if he was locked into some inner battle.

"Yes, two girls, seven and three." He deftly flipped the omelet and put it in a plate.

"I'll pour the juice." Nadine got up, feeling a twinge of disappointment. She was crushing on Brandon. What was more, she hadn't had a major crush since her teens and here she was, having a mammoth-sized crush on a married man with kids.

"If you want, you can stay over at the apartment as long as you want," Nadine said helpfully, after they brought their plates out to the patio. "We are not having any visiting artistes until April. November to February is touring season for most artistes so they usually don't settle down to do studio work at this time."

Brandon was in the midst of cutting his omelet when he paused for a moment. "You are being extremely kind."

"Something tells me that you could use a break," Nadine said to him frankly. She wanted to pry but she was limited by politeness, and Brandon seem to have a big 'keep off' sign on his forehead. Besides, she didn't want to seem nosy.

"I do need a place to stay," Brandon said slowly, "but I am thinking it would probably have to be on the other side of town, possibly closer to my old home. I can't be too far away from my girls. Maybe I could stay with my parents but they would ask too many questions and frankly, I don't know what to tell them about what's going on. They would worry. They are salt of the earth types, you know. They believe that marriage is forever."

"Where do...did you live?" Nadine asked, stumbling over

what to say. She was dying to ask about his marriage. Was it over for good? What happened to drive him away from his home that he couldn't even tell his parents?

"Norbrook," Brandon replied, naming an affluent neighborhood.

"And your wife has custody of the children?"

"God, no." Brandon shuddered dramatically. "I hope it doesn't come to that, and if it does I want custody. I will fight for custody with my last breath."

"So you aren't going through a divorce now?" Nadine asked.

Brandon looked past Nadine and over the foggy morning view and then heaved a sigh. "I don't know. It is likely that there is where I will end up. I grew up thinking marriage was for life. I am even reluctant to say the word divorce."

Nadine nodded. "I understand, especially when children are involved."

Brandon grimaced. "I may not have a choice, though. I don't think I am capable of living with Ashley again. Maybe now is not a good time to talk about this. It's still too fresh."

"Yes." Nadine picked up her juice. "Sorry."

"So what about you?" Brandon asked after a short silence. "Are you going on tour this holiday or are you going to be around?"

"I have ten tour dates with my granddad in Europe in December but that's all I am booked for. I'll be back here for the New Year." Nadine grinned. "They are sold-out tours; people can't get enough of Gramps Langley."

"He's a really good artiste." Brandon nodded. "Love his conscious music, and his responsible lyrics."

"Yeah," Nadine grinned. "He's old school. I tend to go off the same pattern. I was shocked when my single was so well received by the world. You know people are more into the auto tune craze."

"I liked it," Brandon smiled at her, "classic break-up song with just the right hint of melancholy. Were you going through a break-up when you wrote it?"

"No," Nadine laughed. "My ex boyfriend, Sanjay, could not inspire so much emotion in me."

"Sanjay Lewis, the track star?" Brandon grinned. "The tabloids used to call you two the golden couple."

"You read the tabloids, Dr. Brandon Blake?" Nadine raised her eyebrows mockingly. "Somehow you look like you read... er... more serious stuff."

Brandon laughed. "I can dig my head out of the scientific magazines now and then, you know. My wife likes the gossip mags. She says she likes to see what people are wearing; it is good for business. She owns a boutique catering to the well-to-do. When she carries the magazines home, I may take a look in a few of them.

"You have been on the front pages for quite a while now. I may have picked up a magazine or two just to look at you. You are really pretty. You are even prettier in person, which I understand is a rare thing in this age of Photoshop."

Nadine gasped. He said it so matter-of-factly and without hesitation. She searched her mind for a witty comeback but she only managed a squeaky thanks and leaned back in her chair, feeling self-conscious.

He thought she was pretty. What did that mean? Was he feeling the attraction between them that she thought was humming in the air? Why was she even entertaining the thought? Brandon was married and he had not given her any indication that he liked her.

Brandon looked at his watch and groaned. "I am going to have to go. I have a department meeting at eight."

He flashed her a smile. "You know I am getting a wee bit

tired of academia. I am having some trouble juggling my private jobs with my full time job. I just might go back into the private sector after this year."

Nadine nodded, feeling warmed by the fact that he shared that tidbit of information with her.

He stood up and took up her plate at the same time that she stood up and reached out for them as well.

His fingers brushed hers and it felt like liquid fire. She actually looked down at her hand to see if he had something in his hand to generate the heat.

"No, it's okay," she stammered, exhaling when he drew his hand away from hers. "I can't expect you to cook and wash up."

Brandon looked at her, concerned. "You okay?"

"Yes," she said breathlessly, *just move away...far away so that I can get this short circuiting response under control.*

"Okay." Brandon finally moved away. "I might take you up on the offer to use the apartment for a couple of days, until I sort some issues out."

Nadine nodded numbly and then blurted out. "Do you want to have dinner tonight? I mean, I know you don't have any food in the apartment and..."

"Yes, sure," Brandon cut into her babbling. "Thanks, Nadine. I'll be by at seven or thereabout."

He headed through the door in a brisk manner and she watched him, finally sinking down into her chair when he left. Her fingers tingled where his hand touched hers.

Chapter Five

Ashley walked into her boutique, Uptown Couture, later than usual. She had had the most harrowing morning with the children. Ariel had not stopped crying when she had picked her up from her grandmother. She was howling for her daddy all the way to pre-school, and Alisha had looked as if she didn't believe Ashley when she told her that Daddy was away for a while.

"Why didn't Daddy say he was going somewhere?" her daughter had asked her accusingly, as if she knew instinctively that her mother had done something wrong. "Daddy always tells us if he is going away for long. He never just goes!"

"Morning, Ashley!" her store clerk, Jaya, called to her as she headed for the back office through the lush carpeted display area. Already there were several customers milling around; she recognized a few of them.

Most of them were ladies of leisure who were married to powerful men. She murmured a greeting to those who were closest to her and waved to Jaya, pasting on a smile though she did not feel the least bit cheerful, and then hurried to the back office.

Her head was throbbing slightly, a combination of her lack of rest last night and Ariel's squealing this morning. She wished the child had come with a remote control button so that she could press off.

She slouched in her chair and put her head in her hands, disregarding all the yoga and Pilates instruction that she had learned about correct posture.

She felt like crap. Guilty. Weary. She needed a change of life. She had been saying so for years.

She groaned and put her head on the desk, snapping it up again when she heard someone clear their throat at her office doorway.

"Regina," Ashley murmured and rubbed her temples. "What are you doing here?"

"I brought a lawyer. This is Damon. He works at my dad's law firm."

"Oh, for crying out loud!" Ashley looked at Damon, a young guy who didn't even look like he had started to shave yet. He smiled at her apologetically.

"Hi Ashley. Regina said that you really wanted to lead the attack."

"What attack? I am not at war." Ashley glared at Regina. "I think my friend has jumped the gun. My husband and I just had a simple misunderstanding."

"As I see it," Damon came farther in the office and sat down across from her, putting down his briefcase and folding his arms. "You were caught in flagrante, in bed with your lesbian lover. You have to act swiftly, before Brandon does. Make all the moves first."

"You told him everything?" Ashley turned to Regina, her

eyes wide open. "For heaven's sake, Regina!"

"Damon knows about me," Regina shrugged. "I am not in some closet hiding what I really am, unlike you."

"I am not hiding in any closet," Ashley growled. "I am not a lesbian. I date men. I love men. I love my husband. I was only brought into this whole fiasco because of blackmail. You...you..!" She flung her hands up and then looked at Damon mutely. "Regina is the cause of my problems and I think I hate her. No, I know I do."

"Rubbish!" Regina snorted. "I have always been your bit on the side, and you like me."

"Come in and shut the door," Ashley said, slumping her shoulders. "I don't think I want the whole world to hear my business; do you?"

She glared at Regina resentfully. She was once more back in Ashley's life, creating problems and messing with the smooth order of things, blackmailing her and threatening to expose her secrets.

Regina was a prime example of why it was not a good idea to make a deal with the devil. There was no escape until you were sucked dry and left in a pile of destruction. She had tried to shake Regina from her life several times but she was like a parasite, she wouldn't let Ashley go. Regina's strategy over the last eight years was to threaten to tell Brandon her secrets but now Brandon knew at least one of them, and he was not going to forgive her.

She looked at Damon and then blinked away the weak, pitiful tears that were threatening to fall. After the divorce she would get rid of Regina. She would have no fighting chance with anyone else if Regina was in the picture, and she did not want Regina around anymore. She was well and truly tired of her possessiveness and her constant threats.

Ashley glared at her. She had a smug expression on her

face, like she had won some type of prize because she had finally gotten rid of Brandon.

Regina winked at her and came to sit beside Damon, her hand hanging between her widespread legs. She had her hair low in a crew cut and dyed platinum blond, with her name etched into the short sides.

She was very light-skinned and had a tattoo of a rose on her neck and several piercings above her eyelids and nose. Her body was hard, with not an ounce of spare fat, and she usually dressed like a guy in big shirts and baggy pants.

Up until recently she played football for the national team. She still trained with them, even though she had a knee injury. Ashley couldn't believe that Brandon hadn't seen that Regina was a lesbian. It was so obvious; even his sister, Latoya had commented on it once.

Ashley focused her eyes on Damon again. "I came into the marriage with nothing. The house is Brandon's; even this business is his. He pays for everything."

Damon fanned her off. "It doesn't matter, it is marital property. The house is marital property; any money that he has made since you two got together is marital property. To ensure that he continues to pay for your lifestyle, you can request full custody of the kids and then he'll be forced to pay for their upkeep until they are eighteen."

Regina grinned. "It's just like having him pick up the tab without pretending that you love him."

"I do love him," Ashley said, annoyance in her voice. She hadn't even realized how much she still loved Brandon until she had pushed him too far last night. "I really don't want full custody; the kids would be devastated. They prefer Brandon to me. I know that is not something that a mother should admit but that's really how it is at my house. Gosh, this is too much; maybe it would be simpler if I just beg his forgiveness. Tell him that it was a one-off with Regina. Brandon is a true Christian man, loyal and forgiving. He might forgive me."

"Hell no, you won't!" Regina growled. "If you do that I'll tell him the truth about all your little secrets, everything," she said threateningly. "I was before him and I will be after him. You and I can finally get a chance to be together permanently, without sneaking around. Maybe we could go to New York and get married."

Ashley closed her eyes and swallowed. Not if she could help it.

"You will have to request full custody; it will make him more pliable," Damon said, leaning forward earnestly.

There was a heavy silence while Ashley weighed her options. "Let me think it over." She looked at both Regina and Damon. "I haven't even talked to Brandon since last night. It's barely a day. Regina is jumping the gun."

"He's not going to be fighting for your marriage like a ninny after this," Regina sneered. "Get that out of your head and wise up."

"Okay, okay. Give me some time." Ashley felt like kicking Regina and the lawyer from the office. Both of them were giving her a headache.

"All right," Damon got up. "Don't hesitate to call me." He pushed a business card at Ashley. "The sooner the better."

When they both left Ashley put her head on the desk and closed her eyes. She remembered the first time she met Brandon.

It was at church, of all places. She had decided to go because of a near-death experience that had her walking out of a car crash with barely a scratch...

August 2004

It was May and Ashley had just celebrated her twenty-first birthday with a bang. Her father, a sound system selector, had thrown an all-white birthday bash for her in Craig's front lawn, an asphalted place hemmed around with zinc and wood. It was ironic that they called the place a lawn because it had not a speck of greenery. At one end were stacks of black sound boxes, a little off to the side were the sound selectors and a steady stream of people who were coming into the enclosed area, most of them in white.

Ashley wasn't feeling so well. She had developed a slight headache from earlier in the evening and the music and the gaiety felt flat, like she was just an observer and not the main celebrant.

Her father was in his element, spinning on the turntables and giving her shout outs at regular intervals. They were only serving to make her feel even lousier.

"Why are you looking so glum?" Regina danced up to her. "This party is great!"

Ashley plastered a smile on her face for Regina's benefit.

"Here, have a drink," Regina laughed and handed Ashley a beer.

"You shouldn't be drinking." Ashley took the beer and shouted over the music, "You are driving me home later, remember."

"I am invincible," Regina grinned. "It takes more than a few beers to get me drunk."

A girl grabbed Regina from behind and she laughed then turned to her and danced away.

Ashley hugged herself and pressed back farther from the music, which was making her eardrums vibrate. The problem with this type of party was that you couldn't think--couldn't have a decent conversation with anyone around, and she really would not mind a sensible, intellectual conversation right now.

She was suffering from a mid-life crisis at twenty-one because she was so totally and completely depressed about her life so far that she didn't know how she functioned daily.

She wanted more. She had always wanted to do more with her life. So far she hadn't done a thing worth mentioning.

Though she had grown up in one of Kingston's violent inner cities and had no stimulation to learn, she had always been bright. Her high school teachers had called her a genius, though she hadn't been officially diagnosed as one, but she had always known that she was different from the other children around who lived in the poky housing estate where she had lived with her father, her stepmother, and her six half siblings.

She had done exceptionally well at school too, always coming first in her classes. She had taken a staggering thirteen CXC subjects and had passed all of them with distinction. It had coincided with the year that her community had gone through a gang feud.

Her achievements had been remarkable, and she had been featured in one of the national newspapers and touted as the girl who had beaten all the odds to come out on top.

She had gotten two scholarships and went to university and before she could send out applications and fret about returning to live in the cramped two-bedroom place with her father and stepmother, she had gotten a job as a teller in a Merchant bank and shared a flat with another girl who worked at the bank.

Maybe the reason that she was feeling so out of sorts now was because she hated this kind of lifestyle. She looked around at the glistening, sweaty people around her. She sniffed the air heavy with the smell of marijuana and shuddered. She wanted to go home, desperately. Her eyes collided with Jason, her very first boyfriend from high school.

He waved to her casually with a drink in his hand and she waved back. They had parted amicably the year before she went to university.

She didn't know what he was doing at her birthday bash but usually birthday bashes in her father's community were an excuse to make some money. They charged for an entry fee and charged for drinks.

Jason looked like he was pondering coming over to talk but she turned away. She didn't want him to come talking to her and try to resurrect anything. Last time she heard Jason was a drug dealer.

It was ironic; when they were in high school they had thought that they were so in love. Now, they couldn't be more different, and she wondered what on earth she had seen in him then. He was not her type.

Her boyfriends now tended to be ambitious guys who were going places. She hadn't quite managed to catch that wealthy guy that she had been looking for, that millionaire who would sweep her off her feet and out of poverty and into the rarified world of the rich and famous.

Recently she had gotten tired of the dating scene. She was tired of the empty feeling that she got when she spoke to the guys around her.

She felt more for Regina than she did with any guy and that was saying something, because she had a love-hate relationship with Regina.

After years of Regina badgering her about sex, she had done the unthinkable and slept with Regina in her last year of university because she had been cash strapped and desperate. Her scholarship had been halved that year, and she had lost her job at the school library.

Regina had offered to help her, on the condition that they become lovers. She had agreed. She hadn't been bi-curious or anything; she was just desperate for the money.

She still considered herself to be a straight woman. She still loved men. It was just that she hadn't seen a way out then.

Regina was currently paying her rent uptown, making up for her shortfall, so she still slept with her. These days she did it reluctantly; she felt like she was a prostitute somehow. She had become Regina's unwilling slave, and Regina reminded her of her debt to her every day.

She passed the endless zinc fences and headed to Regina's car. She sat in the front seat and breathed a sigh of relief. Maybe she could get some sleep and completely blot out her raging and conflicting thoughts. She wished she could make a new start—wipe her slate clean, have a different life.

She hadn't realized that she had fallen asleep until she heard the car start up and Regina giggle.

"Man, that was a nice party."

"What time is it?" Ashley looked at her watch groggily.

"Time to take you home, Miss Anti-social." Regina backed out of her parking space and onto the road. "Don't bother looking at the car clock. I think it's broken. You slept through your own birthday bash."

Ashley realized that Regina was driving faster than usual but didn't comment.

When they reached stoplights Regina drove through them, whether they were red or green.

"Should you be doing that?" Ashley asked fearfully.

"Nobody follows stop signs in the downtown district at this time of the night," Regina said carelessly. "Close your eyes and go back to sleep."

Ashley closed her eyes and then flew them open again when she heard a loud thud and then felt a sickening jolt.

They had crashed under a truck.

And so she found herself at church the next weekend. Her flat mate's boyfriend invited them to music day at his church, and she was feeling so grateful to God for saving her from certain death that she had gone. Maybe that was why God spared her. What she knew for sure was that somebody somewhere must have been praying for her because she had walked out of the totaled car with only a scratch on her leg. Regina had gotten a couple of deep cuts and broke her hand.

It was a miracle! The firefighters who had come on the scene before the police had asked her what happened, not knowing that she was in the accident.

She sorted through her meager collection of clothes that could be considered modest church wear and had gone to Vintage Road Church in the middle of the town. Her roommate's boyfriend had to find parking quite farther down the road. The church was very well attended and had almost been jam-packed because of the music day. She hadn't felt out of place because there were so many visitors from other churches as well.

It was a good service and she found herself wondering why she didn't do the church thing on a regular basis. She found that she actually felt good. She loved the songs about God and his goodness, his love and his mercy. She found herself pondering after one song that surely God would be merciful to her and deliver her from Regina. She wanted to escape that part of her life. For the first time in a long time, she felt a sort of peace. Maybe Christianity was the answer. Maybe God had chosen the accident to show her what to do.

She had been contemplating that when they had the offertory reading for the collection of the offering and a guy stood up. She must have made a sound because the lady beside her chuckled quietly.

"He always gets that reaction. He looks good, doesn't he?"

"Well, yes," Ashley replied, pretending nonchalance while she stared at him in a sort of trance.

"Don't let his good looks fool you," the lady said, a friendly twinkle in her eye. "He is a genuine good salt of the earth kind of Christian guy. You stand no chance if you are not as holy as he is. He has pretty high standards that don't involve looks, so even though you are pretty, I wouldn't automatically think you have a chance. I know because I have tried. I think almost all the females in this church have tried."

Ashley stared at the guy and then murmured so that only the lady could hear, "What's his name?"

"Brandon Blake" was the prompt response.

Ashley had then gone into makeover mode. She had been a girl on a mission. First, she had found out that Brandon taught a Bible class every Wednesday evening with the new converts of the church or people who were thinking of becoming baptized. Then she had bought a Bible and started to studiously attend the class. She had devoured the Bible like a maniac, bringing herself up to speed on many of its stories so that she didn't appear ignorant before her new Bible studies teacher.

And she loved the studies. She realized that Brandon was a patient and intelligent teacher. Eventually he started to notice her because she asked various challenging questions. He seemed to like that.

She knew she had hit the jackpot when one Wednesday night Brandon asked her, after Bible studies class, if she wanted to go with him to a basketball game: Vintage Road church versus Eastwood Church.

"It is going to be epic." He had smiled at her, his straight white teeth almost dazzling.

After that game she knew that she would love him. It was that simple and that profound. He was fun, he had a brilliant sense of humor and he was as disciplined and as straight shooting a guy as she would ever meet.

She got baptized because of him. She knew that Brandon would not take her as seriously if she was not a church sister. He spoke often about being unequally yoked with unbelievers, and she wanted to have a fighting chance with him. She would have done anything. She had changed her dressing, her hair, her whole demeanor because of him. After he introduced her to his mother, she had tried to emulate her to the point where she was really feeling as if she could be different. She started walking the walk.

She had hunted the church's most eligible bachelor and had succeeded. The night he proposed she had felt as if she were on cloud nine, but she had come thumping down to the ground when she saw Regina at her doorstep waiting for her.

"You can't get married to this guy," Regina had pleaded with her. "It's not right. You belong to me."

"I don't belong to anyone!" Ashley had shouted. "I am no one's possession. Leave me alone!"

"If you marry him, I'll tell him about us." Regina threatened.

"I'll tell him first," Ashley said boldly.

"And will your holier than thou guy understand it?" Regina rasped.

"Shut up," Ashley said, opening her door. "If you say you love me so much, why won't you just let me be happy?"

She slammed the door in Regina's face. Regina had left her alone, only resurfacing after she found out that Ashley had been having an affair with Carlos King at the bank where they both worked.

Regina had always been on the periphery of her life, watching her in fascination as she failed to live up to the ideal woman for Brandon.

It was ironic that after marrying Brandon she had started to resent his gentle, upstanding Christian ways. She had resented him for being so good. His life, his whole demeanor, was like a rebuke to her. Her facade had begun to slip. She had stopped going to church after year one. She just couldn't do the pretense anymore; besides, there had been the affair with Carlos and she had been feeling so guilty every sermon at church seemed as if the preacher were targeting her.

Most days she woke up she felt like a fake and a failure, and she was constantly afraid that one day Brandon would see through her and know. She could see his frustration with her but he had never lost his cool to the extent that she had seen the other night. She shivered uncontrollably. She had gone from the girl who wanted Brandon at all cost to the girl who broke him.

Tears came to her eyes. What had she done? A tight pain wrapped itself around her heart. What on earth had she done?

"Ashley!" Jaya called from the door. "Are you all right?"

Ashley raised her head from her arm. "What is it?"

"Your phone has been ringing and you aren't answering."

"Oh." Ashley glanced at the phone. She didn't hear it ring, so caught up was she in her reminiscing.

"Are you okay?" Jaya asked again.

"No, headache." Ashley shook her head and then winced. "Give me some time."

Jaya nodded sympathetically and left the office.

Ashley breathed in and out raggedly. Maybe she should do the right thing and cut herself out of Brandon's life. She shouldn't have married him in the first place. She hadn't been worthy of him then, and she definitely wasn't worthy of him now. It was time to set him free.

Chapter Six

Brandon stopped by his parents' house on his way from work. Today had been one of the toughest days for him, and he wondered if he should have even gone to work with the way he was feeling.

He was counting down the weeks until the Christmas break and the ending of the contract and then...He didn't know. His whole future felt liquid now. But that wasn't really true, was it? His life had been hanging in the balance for years now, with the constant ups and downs with Ashley. For years he had been overwhelmed by the feeling that his future with her was uncertain.

When he thought about it he realized that he was not as surprised as he should be that Ashley was cheating on him. He had long resigned himself to the fact that the virtuous woman that he thought he had married had all been in his head. It was laughable now that he had gone through Proverbs 30 before they got married and thought that the verses applied to Ashley.

His pastor at the time, Pastor Wiggan, had taken him aside one day after counseling and reminded him, "Charm is deceptive, and beauty is fleeting; but a woman who fears the Lord is to be praised."

He had asked the pastor why he said that and he had replied, "I don't know, Brandon. I have this feeling; maybe it is a prompting from the Holy Spirit. I don't know, but I think that you should reconsider this whole marriage to Ashley."

Too bad Pastor Wiggan had told him that two weeks before the wedding, and he had been so in love, with his head in the clouds. He hadn't had a drop of doubt about Ashley; she had been perfect for him.

They liked the same things; they shared the same sense of humor. They were compatible to a tee and she loved the Lord. Ashley was at every Bible study, every night meeting, sometimes rushing there after work. She prayed like a woman who knew God and loved him.

But it had all been a farce. Pastor Wiggan had prophetic gifts and he didn't even know it. He should look him up and tell him that it was indeed a prompting from the Holy Spirit and it had been a warning for him, one that he hadn't heeded.

He drove into his parents' yard; it was one of the oldest houses on the block in a quiet cul-de-sac near Cherry Gardens. His father had built the house in the sixties. They had added on an extra two bedrooms through the years and the modern and the old blended seamlessly together. It was his very first building project: to blend the old design with a fresh modern one.

He had been ridiculously proud to have done it for his parents, showing off his newly acquired civil engineering skills. The lawn looked immaculate, as usual, and his mother's prized flowers, which she dutifully trotted out to the yearly horticultural shows all over the island, were looking healthy. She still had her first prize Bonsai trees on display on the porch.

A car drove up behind his, and he saw that it was Latoya's.

She jumped out of the vehicle and pointed at him. "Brandon Blake, you had me worried. You left the house the other night and didn't tell me that you were going to leave. I spent all night fretting that I had sent you to the dirty flat when you hadn't stayed there."

"Sorry, wasn't thinking straight." Brandon pushed his hands in his pockets. "Listen, don't tell Mom and Dad about me showing up at your place, okay?"

Latoya laughed. "Really? Don't tell them that you finally had the sense to leave Ashley? You didn't go back to her, did you?" ,

"No." Brandon sighed. "No, I didn't."

"What did she do that was so bad that you would give up your long-suffering, your door matting, your turn the other cheek until she milks you dry stance?"

Brandon wished that he hadn't gone to Latoya's place the night before. She had always encouraged him to leave the marriage. She thought that working things out had been totally one-sided and that he should quit trying to make the relationship work.

She had been right. He looked at her now in her power suit, her hair pulled back in a ponytail that emphasized her sharp cheekbones and her smooth brown skin. Her eyes were shooting sparks.

She was ready to fight on his behalf, as she had always done when they were children. She was just two years older than he was but she was a warrior at heart, usually on his behalf. Judging now from her flashing eyes and her folded arms, she was preparing to do Ashley some harm.

He didn't want her involved. He didn't want anybody to be involved in this. He had to think about Alisha and Ariel. Whatever Ashley was or had done, she was still the mother of his children.

Brandon shrugged. "It's nothing, the regular tiff."

"Liar!" Latoya snorted. "You either caught her in bed with somebody or found her snorting drugs or found out that she was the head of a coven. But I know it's something bad. You have been so busy turning the other cheek for years it has to be something mammoth."

"A coven, though?" Brandon asked. "As in a witch coven? Where do you get these things from, Latty? I thought Ashley was your friend."

"She was, for exactly six months when you first got married, until I realized that she was a pretender. I have been cordial because she is the mother of my nieces, not friendly. Friendly and being friends are two different things. Gosh, Brandy, I can't believe that it took you eight long, long, long years to figure out that she is a fraud. So which one was it? Was it drugs? You caught her snorting cocaine, didn't you?"

"Why does it have to be any of them?" Brandon hedged, turning to lock the car.

Latoya smiled at him knowingly. "So it wasn't drugs, and it's not a coven. She had an affair, didn't she? I always knew she was good for that."

Brandon shrugged.

"You are not going to leave me in the dark," Latoya said threateningly. "I am your big sister. I have to know."

"You two," his mother called from the veranda. "Come look what your father did for me." She headed back inside, a bounce to her steps.

Latoya looked at Brandon. "So you haven't told the parents yet, have you? Because Mommy would not be so happy if you had told her. She likes Ashley for some unfathomable reason."

Brandon shook his head. "Latoya, it was one night. I came to your place to escape. There is nothing much to read into it. Okay?"

Latoya frowned and she walked behind him all the way into the spacious living room, where their mother was standing beside a life-size sculpture of herself. The face of the statue was just like her, in nitty-gritty detail, with a squarish face and wide, deep brown eyes. Even the statue's eyes looked alive.

"It's naked," Latoya was the first one to gasp.

Brandon' eyes hadn't reached the rest of the sculpture yet but when he saw that the statue was indeed naked, with a roundish shape like his mother's, he closed his eyes.

Beatrice beamed. "And he got the proportions right, too."

"I don't think we should be seeing this," Brandon said, struggling not to laugh.

"Oh shut it, you two," Beatrice said, standing back and looking at it. "I did tell him to embellish the bust area a bit. Make it a bit bigger and upright."

"For heaven's sake!" Latoya sat on a nearby settee. "I can't be seeing or hearing this. I am still in my thirties; I could be scarred for the rest of my life. I still have some living yet to do, if God spares my life. I have gone through the first thirty-five years relatively scar-free. Please don't start scarring me now."

"I think that should be scaring not scarring," Brandon muttered.

Beatrice laughed. "I am going to put a dress on it, maybe a long one, or maybe I should just put it in the bedroom."

"Yes, do that," Latoya said. "Keep it far away from prying eyes. It looks so lifelike. I had no idea that Daddy was so good. Where is he?"

"In the basement doing one of the grandkids holding hands. It is going to be awesome."

"I hope they will be clothed," Brandon said worriedly.

"Most definitely," Beatrice laughed and then she looked at Brandon, a serious expression on her face. "I have never in all of my years seen Ariel as miserable as she was this morning when Ashley came to get her. Is everything okay?"

"Ariel is not used to Ashley," Latoya said before he could answer. "Of course everything is not okay. The poor thing is not used to her mother. So before Brandon starts making excuses for his wife, let me just put that out there."

Brandon sighed and looked at his mother. "Well..."

"No defense?" Latoya chuckled. "Finally Brandon is seeing sense and realizing that Ashley is a user and an unfit mother."

Beatrice cleared her throat. "Latoya, you know better than to speak badly of Ashley." She looked at Brandon solemnly. "What's going on?"

Latoya was looking at him too, her eyes bright with questions. "Yes, Brandy what's going on?"

"I hate it when you call me Brandy," Brandon said, deflecting. He didn't want to have to tell them what happened. He stood up and looked through the window in the back yard where his mother had a birdbath. A lone bird was teetering on the edge of the container.

"Mommy, make him answer." Latoya had a wheedling tone in her voice as if she was ten again and her mother could make Brandon do anything.

Brandon glared at her and then turned to his mother. "Ashley and I are going through a rough patch."

"How rough?" his mother asked, sitting down. Her silver hair cupped her chin and swayed a little when she sat down.

He found himself gazing at it for a while. Some of the strands glinted under the weak evening sunlight that was illuminating the hall. He couldn't tell her what happened. His mother was a fairytale pie-in-the-sky kind of person; giving her the sordid details about finding Ashley in bed with Regina would devastate her.

"I think it's an affair," Latoya said while he gathered his thoughts.

"An affair?" His mother raised an eyebrow. "Good Lord, help us. With who? I don't think Ashley is that crazy to have an affair with somebody else. You just don't understand Ashley, Latoya. That's why you don't like her. Try understanding her a little, will you? Instead of judging her."

"Who is having an affair?" His father came up the stairs from the kitchen, wiping his hands on a cloth.

"Ashley," Latoya said with certainty this time, because Brandon was just standing there, frozen at the window. He was contemplating whether to refute what she said or not. Admitting what happened out loud would make it real. He would be putting it out there, and he was reluctant to do so.

"Oh." His father picked up the sculpture and gave Brandon a sympathetic look. "I am going to rectify this," he said, heading back to the basement. "One arm is too large. The face is good but the body is off kilter a tiny bit."

"But Leonard," Beatrice looked baffled, "you act so unperturbed about what Latoya said. Ashley is not having an affair."

"Well," Leonard shrugged, "it's Ashley. She has always struck me as unsettled, like she wasn't too happy with Brandon. She doesn't come to church anymore, she hasn't done so for years, and she dresses like a single woman, like she is on the way to some fashion runway, not to mention how she avoids family gatherings like the plague. In my humble, honest opinion, I thought it was obvious that she was hunting around for someone else. Son, get a good lawyer."

"Leonard!" his mother squeaked. "Who said anything about a lawyer?"

"The boy can finally be free." Leonard put down the statue and looked at Brandon unwaveringly. "Ashley has turned him into a house mom. Their relationship is not a partnership. She isn't a helpmeet. She is a parasite. Birds can't fly on one wing.

"The only good thing that has come out of the marriage is Ariel and Alisha. That's my two cents; sorry if it hurts. I have been meaning to say it for a long time now, but you know that I think parents should butt out of their children's relationships unless they are invited to give their opinion."

He dragged his eyes from Brandon's and looked at Beatrice significantly and then nodded and left the room.

Latoya clapped her hands. "Bravo, Dad! Bravo."

"This is not a concert, Latoya! Leonard!"

Beatrice looked at her husband's retreating back and then at Latoya's smirking face.

She then swung around to him, a confused, fearful look in her eyes.

Curiously, his father's statement was a jolt to him. He had thought that he was the only one, besides Latoya, to notice the blatant disregard Ashley had for him.

However, his father had been keenly observing and had not said a thing. His father operated on a need to know basis. He was not the kind of person to interfere in his business but hearing it so starkly spelled out was jolting, to say the least.

"I know a good lawyer," Latoya said, "Richard's cousin, Kenneth. I am sure he can help."

"Now you just wait a minute there," Beatrice piped in. She was agitated and confused. Brandon could see the crease between her brows and the disapproval stamped on her face.

"Lawyers, divorce—what are you going on and on about? So Ashley had an affair. That does not mean automatic dissolution of your marriage. People work these things out all the time. They get back together and they become stronger."

Latoya was shaking her head vigorously. "Ashley is not good for him, Mom. This is not just some frivolous reason for Brandon to leave. He needs to be free of her and meet a good woman. You know how many friends I have who would be perfect for him, who would love him and be a good wife."

"They have children. My grandchildren," Beatrice said sternly. "Children trump feelings, and yes, I believe that if you have them you should stay together until they grow up and pass the worst." Beatrice turned to Brandon. "This man that she is having an affair with—is it a one-time thing or..."

Brandon sighed. He might as well just tell them the truth. He couldn't have his mother thinking that he was the bad guy for wanting to break up his family. He paused for while before delivering the news. "Well, actually she is not having an affair with a guy."

"You see," Beatrice looked at Latoya triumphantly, "and yet you are quick to jump on the divorce bandwagon. Why are people so quick to talk divorce these days? The first threat of a problem, it's divorce. I don't get it, and to make it worse this divorce epidemic is spreading to the church. Every other couple these days starts thinking divorce as soon as a little problem surfaces. It's as if they have forgotten that there are three people in a marriage, the couple and God."

His mother ran out of steam and sat back in a chair.

Latoya looked at him sharply and then gasped. "Oh my word, Mom. Brandon didn't deny that Ashley was having an affair; he just said it wasn't with a guy. It's her friend

Regina, isn't it? Good Lord, deliver us from all evil!" Latoya clamped her hand over mouth. "As much as I dislike Ashley, I couldn't...didn't imagine this."

Beatrice was still, really still. "Deny this madness, Brandon. Ashley is not a... a..."

"I can't," Brandon shrugged, "I caught them in my bed last night."

Then he found himself telling them the whole sordid story, after which he felt tired, like all the energy had been drained from him. All the pent-up hurt and anger flared up again and then died down, leaving him weak.

His mother was crying. Latoya was soothing her but his mother was having none of it. She got up and went to her room. She slammed the door on a sob and Brandon sighed.

His sigh was the only sound in the quiet room.

"Where are you staying?" Latoya asked him after a long silence. "Obviously it isn't here."

Brandon told her about his encounter with Tara and the offer of the apartment from Nadine.

Latoya widened her eyes. "Nadine Langley? Wow! How is she in person?"

"She's pretty and really kind and easy to talk to." Brandon smiled weakly. "I am supposed to be having dinner with her tonight. I am not in the mood, though. I probably should just do the shopping and crash."

"You mean lie in the dark and curse yourself for marrying Ashley? Maybe you shouldn't be alone now." Latoya came to sit beside him and took his hand. "I'll have the flat cleaned out tomorrow and furnished properly."

"No." Brandon squeezed her fingers. "I need some time to grieve by myself." He stood up.

"You must have seen this coming, or some variation of it," Latoya murmured. "This shouldn't be so devastating; you knew that Ashley wasn't all there in the marriage."

"That I knew but it still hurts like hell. There was always hope, at least on my part, that one day things would get better. That's me, the stupid optimist." Brandon cringed when images of Ashley and Regina in his bed came to his mind. "But not for one moment did I see this coming. I must be dumb. If I couldn't see Ashley for what she was I don't think my judgment is all that good, is it?"

*****

Brandon didn't even stop to get something to eat. He headed straight to the apartment and sank into a living room settee and didn't bother turning on the lights, nor did he answer his phone, though it rang several times. He couldn't rouse himself from his stupor to even attempt to do so. He knew he should call Nadine and cancel but physically he felt incapable of lifting the phone. It was as if he was having a delayed reaction to last night's events.

On the drive from his parent's house he had started thinking about what had happened and then the thought hit him how utterly emasculated he felt. Maybe Ashley hadn't even liked him to touch her. All this time he had thought that even though their relationship was heading down the toilet they were at least compatible sexually. That was the one thing that he could count on, even if they were having bad days.

He never had to beg for sex like some husbands claimed that they had to. That was the one part of his relationship that was functioning and healthy. Ashley was always willing and eager to share her body with him, even if the sex act had lost all intimacy and meaning for him lately. Was that all an act too on her part; had she made love to him and thought of Regina?

He squeezed his eyes shut and waited out the pain that gripped his chest. He must have dozed off, when there was a knocking on his door. He looked at his watch and groaned. It was way past seven o'clock. He looked through the peephole and saw that it was Nadine standing at the doorstep with a concerned look on her face.

He opened the door and leaned on it. "Sorry I couldn't make it to dinner. My situation just began to sink in and I..."

"No, don't apologize," Nadine said. "I think I kind of get it. I bought you groceries."

Brandon sighed and moved away from the door. "Come on in. I didn't want to put you through any trouble."

"You aren't." Nadine walked past him with two bags. "I brought dinner. I hope you like vegetarian."

He sniffed her perfume. Inexplicably, it made him feel calmer. He tried to capture the scent long after she headed to the kitchen.

He walked behind her. "I am really not particularly hungry and I do like vegetarian once it's not fake meat. Why would vegetarians want to fake the very thing that they changed their lifestyle to avoid?"

She looked at him and laughed. "That's a good point."

"Seriously," Brandon grimaced, "why eat mock chicken or mock fish or mock bacon or whatever? Why not eat the real thing? I hate fakery."

She came closer to him, putting a box of orange juice and eggs in the fridge.

"I hate fakery too. I am not a vegetarian, though. I just brought what Lily cooked for dinner. She always cooks vegetarian on a Wednesday."

"Yes," Brandon inhaled her scent. "You smell so good." He opened his eyes again and looked at her. "Your perfume is amazing."

Nadine smiled at him slowly. "Thank you. I made it myself."

"You made it?" Brandon watched as she portioned out the food that was in one container and handed him a plate.

"Let's go eat and I'll tell you all about my secret hobby." Nadine followed him over to the round glass table in the living room and sat across from him.

"At least this is not fake," Brandon remarked after inspecting the food before tasting it, "and it tastes good too."

Nadine smiled. "Thanks to Lily; she is the best cook. I have nightmares about her leaving my employ."

"So tell me about your perfume making." Brandon looked at her while she had her head down. She had her hair slicked back, little curls at her hairline refusing to be tamed. He could see her perfectly formed shell ears. She didn't have on any makeup, and her face looked smooth as cocoa butter except for a mole above her lip.

She looked up at him; her eyes were a light brown. She blinked and they seemed to get darker. He found her fascinating. In the years since he had married Ashley he had not felt this kind of pull toward anyone.

He watched as she licked her lips. His body tightened in pure unadulterated sexual attraction. He was not functioning right. His wife had cheated, his marriage was all but over, and Nadine was being nice to him. That's why he was acting like this. Anybody he spoke to now he would probably find attractive; it just so happened to be Nadine—at least that was what he was telling himself.

Nadine interrupted his thoughts. "One year we were touring Germany and I caught a cold. I bought a small sample of essential oils from a lady who claimed that they would set me right and they did. They really did. " Nadine laughed sweetly. The sound surrounded him and soothed him, like her perfume.

Brandon watched her and thought about the last time he had a conversation with a female who laughed with him, talked to him and did not snarl cagily at the least little provocation. He was liking this.

"So you got interested in oils?" he prompted.

"Yes, and then I realized that some of them smelled really good and they had certain effects on the senses. Like the perfume I am wearing now is a mixture of Lavender, Clary Sage, Geranium, Patchouli, Rose Bulgarian, Sweet Orange, Ylang Ylang and Chamomile. It's nice, isn't it?"

"Very, though I don't recognize a few of those plants." Brandon cleaned his plate and then sat back and watched as Nadine finished her food.

"You must have had an interesting childhood," he said easily.

Nadine nodded. "Yes, I did. I spent most of my time with my grandparents on both sides of the family, and I was Gramps' protégée. We traveled a lot. That kind of experience was good for my career."

"I remember reading about that," Brandon said. "You are a musical genius."

Nadine flushed. "Not a genius exactly. I was just exposed to the right things and pursued it with a single-minded determination for years. I have an ear for sound."

"Modest, pretty, talented and kind," Brandon said softly. He leaned forward in his chair, getting one more whiff of her perfume. "Want us to go on the patio to watch the stars?"

"Sure," Nadine said, getting up. Her hands were trembling a little from his compliments. She hoped that he couldn't see that they were shaking. She was severely attracted to Brandon. It wasn't a fluke. She thought it had been a flash in the pan kind of feeling or maybe it was an intense crush she had on him. She had had several of those when she was a teenager, but that sort of feeling usually died quickly and painlessly.

She picked up the plates and he got up to go to the patio. She was an adult now. This was not merely a crush.

I like you! she wanted to blurt out to Brandon. *I know you are hurting about a breakup and I know that this is lousy timing and I know that I have no business being here, but I like you.*

She didn't say it though. It was too soon to be telling a guy stuff like that, too soon to even be sure that she really liked him. She inhaled deeply before joining him.

They sat on the lounge chairs. Brandon looked up at the starry sky.

"Thank you for being here, Nadine," Brandon said in the quietness. "It has been a rough two days."

"You are welcome," Nadine said softly. They sat and stared at nothing for the longest while, until Nadine told him she had to go.

Brandon looked at her in the half-light, his eyes heavy. "Want to do something tomorrow?"

"Sure," Nadine nodded vigorously. "I have tickets to a play at the Little Theatre. It's starring Oliver Samuels. The clips on television look hilarious."

"That would be nice," Brandon said. "I need a good laugh."

*****

Brandon woke up at exactly five-thirty the next morning, and it took him a while to realize that he was not in his king-sized bed at home. He felt around in the bed. There was no Ashley gently snoring beside him; no sound of the barking dog next door; no rustling of leaves from the tree that was too close to the house that he didn't have the heart to cut down.

There was only the sound of silence and then the low thrumming pain when he remembered where he was and why.

He glanced at his watch. He didn't have to tip-toe to the girls' room to wake them up.

He didn't have to do anything. He was a single man without a family. The thought made him feel bereft and lonely. He loved being there for his girls.

He pulled himself out of bed and got ready. He was running out of clothes. He needed to get more clothes; that meant that he had to face Ashley. He didn't think he was ready for that but he had to go to the house, and maybe in the process get his daughters ready for school.

Thankfully, traffic was almost nonexistent this early in the morning. He looked at his watch when he drove up his driveway; it took him fifteen minutes to make it across town. It was almost six o'clock. There was no yellow car in his driveway. He swallowed the bile when he thought of it. He didn't know if he would ever drive up in his own driveway again and not think about Regina's car parked before the garage.

He let himself into the house and tiptoed upstairs. He pushed the master bedroom open and saw that Ashley was asleep, her silk sleep mask over her eyes. He went to the children's room and woke up Alisha first.

"Daddy!" She opened her eyes slowly and then jumped up. She hugged him, her little arms encircling his back. "Mommy said you would be away for a while. You never told us. You can't just go away and not tell us," she lectured him sternly.

Brandon closed his eyes and squeezed her to him. No he

couldn't just go away and not tell her.

He inhaled. "Go get ready for school; we'll talk downstairs."

She looked at him searchingly. Her big brown eyes had so many questions. She got up, reluctance shouting from every sinew in her body.

Ariel woke up by herself when she heard his voice and held onto him for dear life when he bent to pick her up.

Did children have a sixth sense about what was going on around them? Ariel was acting a little clingier than usual. He contemplated that as he got her ready for school.

He went away for business trips all the time. The last time it was for a whole week. He had left the children with his parents but even so, Ariel hadn't acted like this.

"Listen to me, honey." He looked into her golden eyes. "I love you, okay?"

"Love you, Daddy." Ariel hugged him again. He brushed her curly hair and gave her two ponytails while she chatted away about her day yesterday and her friend Chelsea.

They were eating when Ashley came downstairs, hurriedly. "Oh, you are here." She looked at Brandon, a wide, scared look in her eyes. "I looked for them and couldn't find them in bed. I knew it was late..."

"Daddy's back!" Alisha said smugly, as if all was well with her world again.

"So I see." Ashley looked at him tentatively. "Are you back for good?"

"Not in front of the children," Brandon said abruptly and turned his back to her. He couldn't bear to see her now.

It really was too soon and if it weren't for the children, he didn't know if he could have forced himself back to what he was considering in his mind the scene of the crime.

"You really have to wake up earlier, you know." He glanced at her after a short silence, during which Ashley was hanging her head like a whipped child.

"Yes, I know." She looked up at him with tears in her eyes. "Brandon, I..."

Brandon shook his head. "No..."

He glanced at the clock. He had time to get some clothes and other things. He headed up the stairs. He felt Ashley's eyes burning in his back. He took down a medium-sized suitcase from the storage closet and headed to his closet, where he started packing.

"Brandon," Ashley hissed from the doorway, "we have to talk."

"Yes," Brandon said, not looking up, "but not today, maybe not even this year."

"I think we should get a divorce," Ashley blurted out, her voice trembling. "I know that is where we are headed anyway, and I don't want to prolong this."

She waited for some reaction from him with bated breath. She waited for him to protest. Brandon hated the word divorce.

Brandon looked at her, his eyes flashing. "I don't care. Do whatever, but I want the children to live with me."

Ashley shook her head in denial. A part of her had hoped that Brandon would just forgive her. He was the forgiving type; he had done so over and over through the years, but he was still angrily putting his clothes in the suitcase.

"I can't let you have the kids." They were her only bargaining chips. Brandon could not hold a grudge for long when she had his children, could he?

"Then it won't be an easy divorce, will it?" Brandon said waspishly. "It will be war, Ashley. I am not Mr. Nice Guy when it comes to the girls. Got it?"

Ashley swallowed. "Okay, I understand. Maybe we can come to some sort of arrangement until you calm down and come back home. Where are you staying?"

"Smoky Vale Terrace. Apartment 3," Brandon said. "I'll be there for a while."

"Is it too late?" She licked her lips. "Can't you forgive me and forget that this whole thing happened?"

"I would be mad to get back into this marriage the way it was," Brandon said, "and I don't know if I can forget that I caught you cheating on me in the marital bed with your friend Regina."

Ashley backed away from the door. "I am not a lesbian or anything, it was just...I was just..."

"Sexually confused?" Brandon supplied for her.

"I can explain." Ashley inhaled and then exhaled deeply. "Regina and I go way back but we were never lovers in the early days; it was only my final year of university. I needed money. My scholarship was halved and I...I..."

"I can't listen to this." Brandon zipped up his packed suitcase.

"She helped me with my school fees in my final year and in exchange I slept with her." Ashley started talking hurriedly. "At the time I reasoned that it wasn't really terrible. She was a girl; it wasn't like she was a guy or anything. So anyway, I ended my relationship with her when I met you, but she blackmailed me."

Brandon looked up. "Blackmail, that's your defense? I saw you on top of Regina when I got here. You looked like you were enjoying yourself. That did not look like blackmail."

"No, it's not that..." Ashley shook her head. "She threatens me if I don't make her happy. I had to make her happy."

"And how long have you been making Regina happy?" Brandon snarled.

"I stopped when we got married, and then a couple of years later she started blackmailing me again."

Brandon had an instant headache. He looked at Ashley dispassionately. "This is rubbish. You could have told me this before we got married. See, Ashley, communication… Then Regina wouldn't have had the need to blackmail you and I would not have had the surprise of my life, coming home to find you in bed with her. That's all I have been lobbying for throughout this sham of a marriage. Communication!" he yelled and then yanked the zipper on the suitcase so hard he marveled that it didn't break.

"Listen, Brandon, I will go to the counselor again. This time I will participate. I will show up for meetings; it won't be like the last time."

"Too late. We saw the counselor for two whole years and it didn't help," Brandon said bitingly. "Now I know why. You had another relationship and you were feeling guilty."

He left her standing in the hallway.

He ended up going to work late. He had to explain to the girls that Daddy would not be living at the house but on the other side of town. Ariel didn't understand, really, but Alisha certainly did and she hadn't wanted to get out of the car when he reached the school gate.

"Ali honey, I will be by every morning for school and you can spend weekends with me for now."

"You promise?" Alisha asked, her wan little voice tearing at him.

"Yes, I promise," he said. He was the one who spent weekends with them anyway; he made sure that they had a family outing every weekend and of course, church activities.

Ashley had long weaseled her way out of their weekends, so he shouldn't have a problem getting them.

Chapter Seven

"**T**hat play was so funny," Nadine laughed.

They were heading out to the parking lot after the show. "I can't stop laughing even though it's over."

"It was funny." Brandon half smiled. "The henpecked husband and the demanding wife. Quite an interesting story line."

Nadine looked at him, sobering up. "Uh-oh, you look like you didn't enjoy it as much. Is that why you and Ashley broke up?"

"No." Brandon opened her side of the car and watched as she got in and then went around to his side. "Well, maybe a variation of it."

He looked at her in the half-light. "The wife in the play wanted her husband around all the time. I think Ashley and I had the opposite of that; we grew apart. I wasn't henpecked, but she was demanding. I don't think we even know each other that well. Eight years and I don't know how it has came to this...at least we have the kids."

Nadine nodded. "I have never had a bad breakup. I have no idea what it feels like to be with somebody for that long and then, nothing. Sanjay and I had a thing...he was the rising track star and me the upcoming producer and boy, the media loved it. I barely saw Sanjay in our one-year relationship."

Brandon glanced at her. "Really?"

"Yup." Nadine laughed, "I was on tour for most of last year and it was also a track and field world championship year, so he had to train. What really irks me is that when we agreed that we would part for good, he started getting gold medals in his races."

Brandon grinned. "They said you jinxed him."

Nadine laughed. "Yup. I guess I did."

"Well, you may be somebody else's lucky charm," Brandon murmured. "Don't give up hope."

Nadine leaned back in her seat and smiled. "Thanks Brandon."

The thought that maybe she could be his lucky charm churned in her mind and wouldn't quit. She tried to squash it and turned to him jerkily. "Do you want us to get something to eat? I think I am in the mood for a taco."

Brandon nodded. "Sure. I can't recall the last time I did something like this."

"What?" Nadine asked.

"Just talk, go to a play or even a restaurant. I have been too busy living life to actually live life. You understand what I am saying?"

"Only too well. I went to a concert last year and I said the same thing to Gramps. I go to so many parties and I sing and perform at so many gigs but I haven't really attended a party as a guest for a while."

Brandon nodded. "Both of us need a life."

Nadine grinned. "I am game if you are. We can experience life together and not just be bystanders."

Brandon was about to start the car and then he paused and looked over at Nadine. "We can only do this as friends. No romantic involvement whatsoever. That would be too much of a complication right now."

"Fine. I know." Nadine looked at him lazily. "Totally platonic. I know you are married and you might get back together with your wife."

Brandon shook his head. "I don't think so."

"You don't?" Nadine's heart started hammering. That's what she secretly wanted to hear. "You sure you won't miss her one day and decide to get back with her?"

"Almost sure. Not a hundred percent sure. I really don't know." Brandon started the car. "I haven't prayed about this yet. So far I have been literally just reacting but I'll tell you this: it would be a minor miracle if I got back with Ashley. The past few years haven't been happy ones for me. Who knows what God will say? Maybe he has a different answer."

I hope not, Nadine whispered in her head. *I really hope not.*

*****

"You are acting strange, my girl," Gramps Langley said as soon as Nadine entered the studio, two weeks later. "You are so chirpy and happy these days. I am going to give it a wild guess and say that you found yourself a guy."

"I have," Nadine said, smiling and putting down her backpack in the lounge area of the studio. She looked at her grandfather, who didn't look grandfatherly by any regular standards. He was tall and slim and his face smooth and unlined. He was a Rastafarian whose locks reached his knees.

He currently had it in a turban. He had gone completely raw with his diet, and many people swore that he didn't look a day over forty.

Gramps was sixty. He was eating an orange now and preparing to quiz her. She could see the questions in his eyes but her friend and manager, Tenaj King, came into the lobby at the same time.

"Okay you two, it is two weeks to the tour and you haven't confirmed Jay Steele." She looked at the two of them. "One of you with clout needs to call him; apparently I am too ordinary for his team to talk to me. I am not doing last-minute arrangements for anybody, no matter how famous they are."

"Got you," Gramps said lazily. "But more importantly than confirming with Jay Steele is the momentous news that Nadine has found herself a man."

"Well," Nadine shrugged, "he's a friend. We are friends. Just friends."

Tenaj looked at her knowingly. "Yes, like I was just friends with Leroy and then we got married."

"Well, my... er, friend is already married," Nadine said, avoiding her grandfather's eyes, "and he is... er... going through a bad breakup."

"Mmmh." Tenaj folded her arms. "So you are his rebound girl."

"Married is still married," her grandfather said after a pause. "What is with this rebound nonsense? If I leave Selena tomorrow and leave the marital house, I am still married to her. Any new relationships I may have will still be cheating."

"Yup." Tenaj nodded. "I agree. Don't be the other woman. Don't date a married man unless he is free…completely."

"Jeez. You guys are a bundle of fun today. I just said the guy is a friend, and now I am getting a lecture on being the other woman and the rebound girl. I did not snatch him from his wife, people. I met him after he had an issue with her. We are just... read my lips, just friends. We do fun, innocent things together. We go to plays, watch movies, talk. Is there a rulebook somewhere that says that once a man is married you can't be his friend? Gramps, don't you have female friends?"

Gramps snorted. "You like him as more than a friend. If I had female friends who liked me as more than just a friend, it would have to end. I have been faithful to your grandmother for more than forty years and a big part of that has to do with avoiding female friends." He finished his orange with a flourish. "You are flirting with trouble."

Nadine got up. "Well, thank you for that enlightening conversation. Can we talk about the tour? Equipment, et cetera, hotels booked, bands booked, business things--things that do not relate to my private life. You guys are implying that I am a home-wrecker and I don't like it."

"Defensive much?" Tenaj said huffily. "I want to meet this guy that you are so hung up on."

Gramps got up. "Me too. I have never seen Nadine get so hot under the collar about a man before and I mean, even with the track star, she was a little subdued but this married guy has her in knots."

"Argh!" Nadine ran her fingers through her hair. "I can't stand you two."

"Seriously." Her grandfather raised his brows. "Invite him over to the studio. Let him see where you work. Bring him to meet us."

Nadine frowned. "Why would I do that? Why would I subject him to the scrutiny of the two of you?"

"Why not?" her grandfather smirked. "He's just a friend, isn't he? You bring your friends here all the time."

"Okay. Whatever. Fine," Nadine said. "I'll invite him

over."

"What does he do?" Tenaj asked when they were heading to the boardroom. "He is not a singer, is he? I really hope not. I don't know how on earth I am going to spin this for the press if they find out. You have a reputation as a good girl; a home-wrecker would be a bit much for the public to swallow."

"No. He's an engineer, and I am not a home-wrecker!"

"Nice, that's a nice career." Tenaj sat at the head of the table in the spacious boardroom. "What's his name? How old is he?"

"You do not question me about any of my other friends like this." Nadine smirked.

Gramps was pretending indifference but he sat down across from her at the twelve-seater table, his hands crossed contemplatively.

"Okay." Nadine leaned back in her chair. "His name is Brandon Blake; he is thirty-three. "

"Brandon Blake." Tenaj tapped her hand on her forehead contemplatively. "I always love a good first name as a last name, especially when it's a guy. I wonder if he is related to Ashley Blake? She owns Uptown Couture."

Nadine gasped. "His wife's name is Ashley."

"Small world." Tenaj looked at Nadine, a contemplative look on her face. "Very small world."

"What," Nadine asked, "do you know something about her?"

"Not really," Tenaj said slowly. "It's probably nothing. She's, er, how should I put it, really well-polished looking. She always looks like she has walked off the pages of a magazine."

"What do her looks have to do with anything?" Nadine asked. "I am not in competition with her."

"Sorry, I know," Tenaj said, repentantly. "Her husband is just your friend; I don't know why I said that. Anyway, I was thinking of getting some dresses for you for the show at her store."

"Seriously?" Nadine squeaked. "What about our usual places?"

"Nobody has clothes like Uptown Couture," Tenaj said emphatically. "And I mean nobody in all of Kingston, if not Jamaica. Now I wish I never said a thing because you are going to veto her store and I already have the outfits picked out for your opening night."

"No, I am not going to veto it," Nadine said, a half-smile on her face. "I want to go and try out those outfits. Would today be all right?"

Gramps sighed. "Women. There she goes to check out the competition, and she swears this guy is just a friend."

*****

Uptown Couture was on a cul-de-sac off Seventh Avenue at the very end of the road. There was a neat little sign at the gate with a picture of a lady with a bag.

"Where it's hard to be drab," Nadine read from the sign.

Tenaj laughed. "Yup. You do know that you coming here is unorthodox, right? She would have sent the pieces that I want and then you would try them on from the comfort of the studio, like we do with everybody else."

Nadine chuckled. "Relax. I just want to see her, the lady who is crazy enough to let Brandon slip through her fingers."

"Maybe Brandon is the one who let her slip out of his fingers," Tenaj countered. "You have not seen Ashley. Why would a man give up such a gorgeous woman?"

"Brandon seems like the person who is more about

character than looks." Nadine slammed the car door shut.
"He is lovely. He is the perfect man. He is warm and kind
and considerate and handsome and perfect."

"And married." Tenaj injected into her list. "Don't forget
that bit."

"I can hardly do that with you reminding me every two
seconds, can I?"

"There are always two sides to every story," Tenaj said, a
warning tone to her voice. "So Brandon maybe warm and
kind and sound like an angel dropped from the skies for
you, but has he told you why his wife kicked him out of the
house?"

"No." Nadine sighed. "I don't think she kicked him out, I
think he left."

"He hasn't told you and you are such good friends," Tenaj
snorted. "Usually if they are not spouting off the faults of the
wife, it's their fault."

"Oh, for goodness' sake," Nadine hissed. "Brandon is not
the kind of person to be talking bad about anybody, and he is
not the type to confide in me about his private business. I like
and respect that about him. Well, I kinda hate it too, because
I really want to know what went down. He implied that they
had grown apart."

"Yeah, right, 'grown apart'," Tenaj said. "Forgive the
cynic in me, but nine out of ten times, marriages break up
because of the man. And don't they have kids? Why would
he leave the house with his wife to care for the kids alone,
just because they are growing apart? Selfish beast, he should
be concentrating on bridging the gap in his marriage, not out
pretending to be a single man with you."

"He goes to the house every morning to get his children
ready for school. He takes them to school; he spends the
weekend with them. He's a good dad," Nadine offered in his

defense, "a very good father. I have never seen anyone love their children more. So I surmise that in this case it's the wife that's the cause of the problem. Not him. Don't you?"

Tenaj grunted. "I don't know about that."

"You are so quick to defend the wife aren't you?" Nadine asked as they headed toward the entrance to the store.

When they opened the door they saw that the inside was completely done in red carpet. There was even a section at the back that was set up like a red carpet event with different clothing brand names printed on a backdrop.

The place looked and smelled exclusive.

A girl who was dressed in an expensive looking cut jacket suit approached them with a smile on her face. Nadine might not be that familiar with the trends in clothing, but she could see that the material wasn't cheap.

"Hi, I am Jaya. How may I help?"

Tenaj smiled at Jaya, "I called Ashley earlier concerning outfits for a tour."

"Oh, please have a seat," Jaya said, leading them to some plush chairs in front of a wall length mirror.

"Nice to meet you, Miss Langley," Jaya said, looking at Nadine and nodding. She then hurried along the passageway.

Nadine's smile slipped as soon as Jaya turned away. She was feeling a teeny bit anxious to meet Brandon's wife.

She squeezed the end of the chair. How had she gotten so involved with Brandon? She had resolved to just be his friend, but her heart was not cooperating with her mind. Over the weeks she had realized that she was fooling herself into believing she could be a platonic friend. Brandon was so lovable. He was easy to talk to, and the truth was she found herself confessing things to him that she hadn't even told Tenaj, who was her best friend.

He was a listener but he talked to her too, about his family, his parents, his older sister Latoya, and his kids. He never spoke about Ashley, and she never asked.

He had not given her any indication that he thought of her as anything more than a friend. One or two times she had thought that she had caught him looking at her contemplatively, but that had been wishful thinking.

And then there was that time last week when they had gone to the Jazz Lounge to listen to a friend of hers sing. They had seen a couple from Brandon's church and he had introduced her as his friend, but he had kept a hand firmly clamped to her waist. It felt right. It felt a little more than friendly but maybe she was just oversensitive to these things, her overactive imagination wanting there to be more from him than there was.

Her first glimpse of Ashley Blake intruded upon her uncomfortable thoughts.

"Oh my word," she whispered, when she saw the statuesque woman with the honey-toned skin and the perfect body striding out to meet them.

"Told ya," Tenaj whispered. "Modelesque."

"Barbie doll," Nadine whispered back.

"Caramel Barbie," Tenaj chuckled, standing up to greet the perfectly turned out Ashley, who was dressed in a no-doubt expensive black dress. Nadine never paid attention to what people wore in terms of cost, but the thing fit Ashley like a glove, emphasizing every perfect contour of her body and highlighting her glowing skin. Ashley and Tenaj air-kissed in the totally fake manner that Nadine hated.

Nadine stood up too and smiled as Ashley turned to her and took her hand eagerly in a handshake. Her eyes, which were heavily eye-lashed and the color of pure warm honey, lit up when she saw her.

"It is not every day we have a celebrity in our store!" she

said. Her voice had just the right hint of huskiness. "I am so excited. I would love if you could autograph something." She smiled, showing off perfect teeth.

Nadine smiled back, feeling a little less pretty than she was this morning. She was telling herself to snap out of it. She usually didn't compare herself to other women, but Ashley Blake was stoking the green-eyed monster.

She listened as Ashley talked to Tenaj about the outfits. They followed her to a private room, where she had the outfits on hangers.

"So which city are you going to first?" Ashley asked excitedly, flipping her thick, almost sable black hair over her shoulders. Nadine was left wondering if her hair was real.

"Paris," Nadine smiled, still looking at Ashley's gleaming hair; if it was fake it was a very good fake.

"I envy you," Ashley said, not a hint of envy on her face. "I went to Paris four years ago and it was superb."

Nadine nodded. Had she gone with Brandon? She was burning to ask. She was never good at fishing for information but she made a paltry attempt anyway.

"They say it is a place for lovers; unfortunately, I'll be working. You must have had a great time with your, er... significant other."

Ashley shook her head. "Actually, I didn't go with my husband. It was a fashion week event and I went alone."

She stood up, as if the subject was not one she wanted to pursue any longer. "So you should try on this red dress." She handed a dress to Nadine. "Tenaj said that your concerts will be recorded, so you need to look great in your outfits."

Nadine nodded. "Only one night will be televised. There are quite a few other famous reggae acts joining us that night."

"Cool," Ashley said, "and then which other cities will you

go to?"

Nadine pointed to Tenaj. "She is the best person to ask."

Ashley turned to Tenaj, who was trying her best to blend into the furniture and watching them interact.

Nadine went into the spacious dressing room and stood for a minute, just looking at herself in the mirror. Had she always been this short, her hair's natural curls so frizzy, her slim body so boyish?

"Snap out of it, Nadine." She whispered. "Snap out of it. She is his wife, the mother of his children. You are just a friend. Just a friend. No need to compare."

*****

When they left the store an hour later, Nadine was quiet.

"So?" Tenaj said as soon as they sat in the car.

"So she's effervescent, bubbly, drop-dead gorgeous," Nadine said mournfully. "She doesn't seem to be going through a breakup though," she added hopefully. "Maybe she doesn't love him and isn't hurting and is happy that he is gone."

"Another woman's trash is your treasure," Tenaj laughed and then sobered up when she saw Nadine wince. "Okay, sorry. That was uncalled for. I don't think Ashley would be crying and blabbering about a breakup. You are a client. She is very professional."

"I know." Nadine sighed. "Is that even her real hair?" She dragged her fingers through her short curls and looked in the overhead mirror.

"Yes," Tenaj said, looking at hers as well. "All hers. No fillers No weaves. I asked. She made me feel it down to her scalp."

"And that shape. I look like a boy compared to her."

Tenaj laughed. "Yes, she is very endowed breast-wise. She has four times the tits you have."

"And her butt is shapely, like she works out."

"Pilates," Tenaj replied, "She goes almost every day. She told me that she can't function without it."

"Okay, I get it." Nadine cut her eyes at Tenaj. "Rub it in. But it doesn't change the fact that she did something that made her husband unhappy. Her perfect, unblemished skin clearly could not save her marriage."

"Clearly," Tenaj said, "but what wouldn't I do for that hair?"

"And that shape," Nadine said on a sigh.

"Okay, enough of the moping and covetousness," Nadine said. "Where to next?"

"Next, we go to Jay Steele and confirm him or not. I am not going to be running around like a headless chicken getting things done for him."

"Okay," Nadine said absently. For some strange reason she was picturing Ashley walking down the church aisle. It had to be a church, because Brandon was a stickler for that kind of thing; she didn't see him getting married on a beach or any other venue. She imagined Ashley in her wedding finery, her hair bouncing on her shoulders as she glided down the aisle, smiling at Brandon with plump lips.

She could see Brandon turning to her with a smile on his face, a look of love in his eyes. *I'll cherish you forever, Ashley*, she imagined him saying.

Tenaj pinched her when they slowed down at a stoplight. "What?"

"What do you mean what?" Nadine asked, irritated.

"You groaned," Tenaj said. "Not feeling well?"

"Nope. I think I am jealous." Nadine groaned again. "I am going to have to stop hanging out with Brandon as a friend.

I really don't think of him as one, and I don't think I can pretend any longer. I think I am falling for him."

Tenaj nodded. "I could have told you that. It's also a good idea to protect yourself. It's early days yet. If you nip this crush of yours in the bud, your problem will be solved in no time."

"So I won't call him or contact him while I am away for the three weeks on the tour. I won't care what he is doing for the Christmas holidays or anything like that."

"Good." Tenaj nodded again.

"I won't even think about him," Nadine said determinedly. "Not even once. I am going to actively find myself a guy that I can grow to love. There is more than one fish in the sea. This guy has to be single, no wife, no ex-wife, no kids no baggage."

"That's my girl." Tenaj gave her a thumbs-up. "Never... ever... ever... be anybody's rebound girl ever... ever."

"Yeah," Nadine said, "I got that, loud and clear."

Chapter Eight

Brandon was on his way from work Friday afternoon when Ashley called. He contemplated not answering the phone but he needed to pick up the children for the weekend and so far she had not raised a murmur when he went for them. This was his third weekend alone with them. They didn't seem to mind it. They liked the apartment so far. He had kept them occupied with church and then two Sundays on a row he had brought them over to his mother's place. They always loved their grandma's place and cooking. So the arrangement was working out for all of them so far.

He again wondered what Ashley wanted as the phone trilled again. He picked it up and answered gruffly. He had not quite managed to reign in his bitterness when he spoke to Ashley, and he didn't expect to do so anytime soon. So many things reminded him of her betrayal.

"Hey," Ashley said huskily, "is it okay if we talk this evening? My mother is in town and I wanted to go to her place for the weekend. She wants to see her grandkids."

Ashley and her mother had recently started building back their relationship after years of estrangement. She was slowly getting to know her grandchildren and though he wanted to protest, he would not.

Ashley's mother was a pretty decent person. Her mother was a believer and he was hoping that through contact with her Ashley could rediscover the relationship that she had once had with God.

He gripped the phone closely and said with a sigh, "I am close to your store. I'll stop by now."

"Cool," Ashley said and hung up. He met up on traffic on Waterloo Road but instead of his usual custom of turning on the radio and listening to a program, he decided to seriously talk to God instead.

He had talked to Him about his situation over the past few weeks but he had been a bit more accusatory than humble. He had asked God why on earth he had allowed him to get married to Ashley. She could not have been the right person for him. He had been thoroughly deceived by her? why had God allowed that to happen?

Surely Ashley had not been a real Christian. She had just visited church in order to hook him. The moment they got married, she had slowly started to wean herself from Bible study, evening devotions, and even wanting to go to church.

Their first argument had been about her not wanting to go to church. She had made up a million and one excuses and it had gotten to him and he had finally confronted her about it.

Not wanting to go to church was for him a symptom of an even greater problem. She was not interested in God anymore. Maybe she had never been.

As a Christian that had hurt him to the core. He had always wanted a wife who was God-fearing, especially since they had children. He wanted them to grow up as Christians and see Mommy and Daddy going to church together and being united. It had been his dream. Instead, what he got was Ashley.

He thought about it now, the first time he had seen her in church. He had noticed her the minute she had walked into the sanctuary with her thick wavy hair bouncing with every step she made. She was in a modest pink dress and a ridiculously tall shoes that had elongated her legs and made it seem as if they went on forever. She had stridden confidently toward the front pew behind an usher.

That day the church aisle had been her catwalk. He had admired her because she was beautiful, and then he had ignored her because he surmised that she was just a visitor, probably a party girl. She certainly looked the type.

When she had kept on coming to church and even Bible studies, he had felt optimistic that maybe he had read her wrong.

When she started participating he had been more than a little surprised that she was so knowledgeable about the Bible. Most of the unmarried guys at church had shown an interest in her by then, but she had seemed interested in him alone and he loved that and reveled in it. In a sense he had felt proud of the fact that Ashley had chosen him.

Pride goeth before a fall...and he had fallen. He had done the requisite counseling but he had already made up his mind to marry her. He could have waited. He should have waited.

Eight years later he could now see with hindsight that he had rushed into the marriage without knowing all the facts, like the glaring one: Ashley had sex with girls. That would have surely posted a red flag somewhere, and maybe he wouldn't have been as quick to jump into marriage with her.

He pulled up in front of the store after reminiscing about

the several bad parts of his marriage. He realized after rehashing their problems that he was not in the frame of mind to face Ashley.

He entered the store with a frown on his face. It was fairly crowded. He headed to Ashley's office, waving to Jaya on his way there. The door was ajar and he went in. Ashley was on the phone. She looked up at him and smiled as if they didn't have a care in the world, as if he hadn't caught her in bed with Regina. As if all was well between them.

He scowled at her some more and noticed that her hands trembled a bit as she put down the phone. *Good.* He wanted her to fear him. He wanted her repentant.

She cleared her throat. "Well, um, hey again."

"Hey" was his laconic reply. "You look well," he said reluctantly. She really looked good today. It didn't move him much, though. Looks, he had quickly found out, could be deceiving. Especially hers.

"Thanks." She cleared her throat. "We were visited by a celebrity today. Nadine Langley."

Brandon stiffened. "Is that so?"

"Yes. She is using our outfits for her European tour. Isn't that something?" Ashley gushed.

"Okay." He didn't comment further. He was having a mixed bag of reactions to Nadine these days. On one hand she was the perfect person to help him forget the debacle that his life had become. He was determined to treat her as a friend, but on the other hand he realized that he was developing feelings for her.

Maybe his feelings were a side effect of his breakup with Ashley but sometimes he found himself wanting to kiss her, wishing that they were the ones together and not him and Ashley. The feelings had gotten so overwhelming over the past week that he was planning to move out of the apartment.

He felt as if he had overstayed there. He was going to actively find himself another place on Monday.

Nadine was the opposite of Ashley in disposition. She was like a breath of fresh air. She was so easy to be around. She was calmer, sweeter, less self-conscious and...

"So what do you think, Brandon?" Ashley asked.

He zoned back in. "Sorry, I didn't get that?" Brandon murmured.

"I started seeing a Christian counselor on my own to work out some of my issues. Believe it or not, I realize that what is wrong with this marriage is me. I am not a good wife or mother."

Brandon leaned forward. "Say that again?"

"I am not a good wife or mother," Ashley said earnestly. "I know that and I am willing to change."

"Have you gotten rid of Regina," Brandon snarled "or are you still trying to make her happy?"

Ashley shuddered visibly. "I have gotten rid of her. She is no longer an issue."

"Really?" Brandon raised his eyebrows. "Why?"

"Well," Ashley shrugged, "it is all out in the open now. My past with her. There is nothing else for her to blackmail me with. I am trying, Brandon. Can you please meet me halfway?"

A revulsion rose up in Brandon and he growled. "How long were you sleeping with her before I found out?"

"Sporadically through the years," Ashley said honestly. "She has always had other relationships and then when they break up she finds me and torments me."

"I don't know if I want to be with you again," Brandon said harshly. "Ashley, you were a nightmare to live with. You are right; you were not a good wife or mother."

"Because I had that secret I was carrying around. I don't

anymore. I am willing to change. I am even going to start going back to church."

Brandon got up. "Don't change on my account, Ashley. Change because you want to. Don't go back to church, either, because you think that is what I would want. Do it because you have a relationship with God and want to meet with his people. Have a nice weekend. Tell your mom hi."

"What are you doing for the weekend?" Ashley asked, her voice tremulous.

It gave him pause. He could not in recent memory remember Ashley caring about anything that he did.

He looked at her, a frown on his face. "Why are you asking?"

"I am just interested, Brandon. Jeesh, you are acting as if I asked some top secret question."

"I was planning to take the kids to the north coast. Richard's beach house in Negril."

"Maybe we can do that next week, then?" Ashley said tentatively.

Brandon paused, his hand on the door. "What? Ashley, I don't think..."

"I am sorry for what happened. I am sorry for what I did." Ashley looked at him. "But I realize that I can't just let us go, Brandon. There was a time when we were good together. I want back that time."

"That is so typical of you," Brandon said softly. "You do something wrong and you think that the whole world should just rush to forgive you. You didn't just bang my car or misplace my keys, Ashley. You cheated on me with another person, in our home. That shows disrespect; it shows disregard; it shows a lack of moral fortitude. Saying I am sorry while batting your eyelashes is not going to cut it with me." He opened the door. "Bye."

"You could meet me halfway," Ashley said, raising her voice. "You just don't want to. What about the kids, Brandon? They need two parents."

"What about trust, Ashley?" He spun around and confronted her wrathfully. "I may never trust you again with anyone, male or female, and don't you dare throw the kids into this; you conveniently remember them only when it suits you."

Brandon left the building as fast as he could. He let himself into his car and drove out of the parking lot so fast the gravel caused his car to skid.

*****

Nadine was leaning on her car and waiting for Brandon in the parking lot when he got back. She was dressed in hiking boots and had a denim jacket thrown around her shoulder.

Brandon, saw her and immediately his sour mood lifted. She smiled at him tentatively, and that worried him. Nadine was not a tentative sort of person. She gave him a little wave and then pushed herself from the car.

"You are a sight for sore eyes," he greeted her happily.

"I am going to my grandparents for the weekend," Nadine said brightly, "I came to give you the essential oils that I promised because I won't be around."

"Your grandparents in Blue Mountain, huh?" Brandon said interestedly. "They are the ones who own the B and B where Tara is staying?"

"Yup." Nadine nodded. "I have to go check on Tara. She sent me an SOS; said she was dying of boredom and other inexplicable ailments."

Brandon chuckled. "I won't be having the kids this weekend. Maybe I can come along. A peaceful weekend in the mountains sounds like a good prescription."

"Sure." Nadine nodded her head. "I could tell my grandparents to prepare a cabin for you. It's cabin style."

"Sounds nice," Brandon said. "Want to wait for me while I pack?"

"Sure," Nadine said and then she frowned. "I was, er, going to tell you that we can't see each other as friends anymore."

Brandon swung around to face her. "Really? Why?"

"I... er... went to your wife's store today and it hit me that you are married. Honest to goodness married. It's not just a theory. You are not divorced, not even really separated. You have a flesh and blood wife who is gorgeous and pleasant, and I..."

She cleared her throat. She chickened out at the last minute. She couldn't tell him that she had feelings for him that she thought ran deep and that she was preserving her sanity.

That would completely spoil the dynamics of their relationship. It would cause awkwardness and stiffness when there was none.

She feared that she was acting like a foolish teenager and Brandon might not feel the same way.

Brandon inclined his head to one side. "And you?"

"And I kind of feel uncomfortable about it. I don't even know if you are going to get back with her."

Brandon sighed. "You don't want to be my friend anymore because I am married?"

"Well, yes... er... no. I can't."

"So maybe I shouldn't come on this trip to Blue Mountain, then?" Brandon said forlornly.

"Well, yes, I mean no. For heaven's sake, Brandon, why did you break up with Ashley? She's gorgeous!" Nadine looked at him anxiously. "Was it something that you did?"

Brandon laughed harshly. "No. I was a relatively good husband. I guess. Maybe I wasn't the best husband for someone like Ashley. Come on inside while I pack. That's if you want me to still come?"

"Yes, sure," Nadine said jerkily. "Sorry to ambush you like that."

Brandon half smiled. They didn't start talking again until they were on the road, heading through Papine and toward the lush green mountains in the distance. Her grandparents had an inn that was midway to Blue Mountain Peak, in Whitfield Hall. Nadine drove and Brandon sat in the passenger seat looking through the window contemplatively.

"Ashley cheated." Brandon spoke after a long while. He had a somber tone to his voice. "That's in answer to your earlier question. That's why I left her."

Nadine looked over at him, a surprised look on her face. She then hurriedly looked back at the road. "Wow."

"Yes. Wow." Brandon grimaced. "It wasn't the best of times for me. I am still thrashing around in my mind as to what to do about the whole thing."

Nadine gripped the steering wheel harder. "Do you still love her?"

It had to be asked. She had so longed to ask that question that she anxiously waited for his response, but Brandon seemed as if he was a million miles away. They were passing by Blue Mountain Inn and heading toward Mavis Bank before he spoke. That was twenty minutes into the drive. Twenty whole minutes while she wondered if he was going to answer, fretting that he would say, "Yes, Nadine. I still love Ashley, with my whole heart."

"I don't know," Brandon finally answered. "I lost that in-love, warm fuzzy feeling for Ashley a long time ago. Our marriage has been on a collision course for so long. That doesn't mean that I don't love her anymore, though. I made up my mind to love her when we said our marriage vows and I will always love her because she is the mother of my children."

"Yes, there is that." Nadine murmured, feeling a tad nauseous. "Some girls have all the luck." She laughed uneasily, trying to dislodge the queasy feeling that his statement brought on.

What did she expect Brandon to declare, how awful Ashley was for cheating on him and that he hated the ground she walked on? That had never been his style and frankly, she wouldn't have found him attractive if it was.

He never bashed Ashley in the month since she had met him. He had only told her why they broke up because she had practically begged him.

He was looking through the window and she wondered what he was thinking. Brandon had times when he became introspective. She understood that much about him and she was respecting his space but it hurt just a tad bit to hear him say that he made up his mind to love Ashley. Who did that? Who made up their mind to love somebody even though they did you wrong?

*****

Do you still love her? The question kept ringing in Brandon's head even when he and Nadine had engaged in another conversation. He had given an answer but really, did he still love Ashley? He tried listing Ashley's virtues in his head but he kept coming up short.

On the other hand, he could list a ton of virtues for Nadine without even trying. If he ever got the chance to do it over, the whole marriage and family thing, he would want it to be with her.

He shouldn't be thinking that way. He hadn't even known

her for a month, but he felt that he really knew her, like finally he had found his soul mate. It was a deep sense of certainty. But he couldn't trust it. He couldn't trust his instincts where women were concerned. Look where leaning to his own understanding got him. It got him Ashley.

He looked through the window at the various shades of green on the mountainsides. The air got cooler the higher they climbed into the mountains.

"Your mom grew up here, in the hills?" Brandon asked a solemn-looking Nadine.

"Yes," Nadine glanced at him. "My dad stayed at the B and B at Whitfield. She was a young girl, barely seventeen, working the front desk then. My dad was visiting with a group from college and then the rest is history. They lived happily ever after—well, until they got divorced, anyway."

Brandon grimaced. "Tara took it badly and that's how I met you. How did you take the divorce?

"I saw it coming." Nadine sighed. "They hadn't been happy together for quite a while, from when I was a pre-teen. They were trying to hold the marriage together for my sake, and then they had Tara. She was the makeup baby they had to help secure the marriage, but of course that didn't work. It never works, so maybe you shouldn't plan a makeup baby with Ashley."

Brandon groaned. "That's the farthest thing from my mind."

"Good." Nadine smirked. "And then one day my parents couldn't pretend anymore," she murmured. "They trudged on for ten years. I was twenty when it happened but it still hurt. Children never really get over their parents divorcing, no matter how old you are."

Brandon nodded. "I know. That's really..." he paused and sighed again, "I know."

Nadine twisted her lips. "I was going to say... at first. People do adjust after a while. I am okay with their other partners now but at first I was resentful. I don't like that kind of change but my mom and dad seem truly happy for the first time in years.

"My dad's wife, Heather, has three girls. They lost their father in a car crash. They are sweet girls. One of them is Tara's age but Tara is so possessive she doesn't want them calling her father Daddy, nor does she want him to give them any attention, which is impossible; our dad is a loving kind of person. Heather is a psychologist; you may have heard her on the radio. She has her own family program."

"Yes." Brandon nodded. "I have heard of her. She has her own set of problems at home, as a stepmother, doesn't she?"

"Yup." Nadine grinned, "Tara is the stepchild from hell. Her skills as a psychologist have really come in handy."

"If I divorced Ashley now," Brandon mused, "my children would not get the chance to be bratty to a stepmother. They would be used to her by the time they were Tara's age."

Nadine looked at him sharply and then the car dropped in a pothole. She cursed under her breath and slowly drove out of the thing, which seemed like it was a mile wide.

"These mountainous roads are pretty, awful aren't they?" Brandon chuckled. "They can cause a perfectly good Christian to curse."

Nadine groaned. "It's not the roads. You said...never mind. Never mind."

Chapter Nine

Brandon was convinced that Nadine was the master of understatement when she said that her grandparents owned a bed and breakfast type inn. He was expecting a quaint little place off the beaten track, probably with a little sign hanging up at the gate announcing that it was open for business. He hadn't expected that they ran a bed and breakfast on a coffee farm.

"An honest to goodness Blue Mountain coffee farm," he whispered, looking around the vast estate. The road leading up to where Nadine indicated was the main cabin was paved. Flanking the walkway were strawberry patches. The scent of strawberry was the first thing that he noticed. He could even spot some strawberries among their white blossoms. He could also see the rows and rows of coffee in the distance.

"I love it already," he said to Nadine. "Somebody should sentence me to live up here."

Nadine laughed. "And you haven't seen Grandma's

greenhouse yet, or Grandpa's grape vineyard. Everything eaten here was grown here."

"Are you sure that we are still in Jamaica?" Brandon asked, chuckling.

"Yes, we are." They walked up to the main building and a little bell chimed as they stepped through the entrance. Inside was done completely in wood and looked rustic.

Tara was around the desk on a chunky computer. She looked up with a bored expression on her face but when she saw them her face lit up.

"Nads! Brandon! Welcome to the sticks! The back of beyond. The place that is going to kill me!"

Nadine laughed and hugged her sister as she hurled herself on her. "I hope you don't greet the guests this way."

"Nah," Tara said, hugging her back, "just filling in for Georgia while she takes a break. I am waiting to see Gersham."

"Gersham?" Nadine looked over her sister, who was almost glowing. The mountain air and the healthy organic food were having a good effect on her.

"Yes," Tara said excitedly, "Gersham Pottinger. They came by this morning with his church group. He is one cute guy, I tell you. His one downfall is how much he loves this place but I can work with that. They are going to see the sunrise at the peak on Sunday. I want to go but Grandma said no.

"I am telling you, Nads, Grandma is not as nice as she used to be. She is strict and mean and she is treating me as if I am ten. Grandpa is not so bad but he is always on the farm. He gives me long lectures about coffee and other boring farming stuff. He said I remind him of Mom when I was her age. Seriously... Uh."

Nadine looked at Brandon, who had wandered over to the wall looking at pictures.

"That's you," he turned to them and grinned, "when you were a little girl."

"Yes," Nadine nodded. "I used to love it up here, unlike Tara. I used to beg my parents to send me here."

"Are you sleeping with him?" Tara whispered in Nadine's ear,

"No," Nadine whispered back. "He is still married, and unlike you, I am old-fashioned. You know, I have this bee in my bonnet that I should wait for the right guy and marry him before we become intimate."

"Yes you are old-fashioned," Tara snickered. "You would fit right in with Granny's old country church set. I personally can't stand them. Nads, they have these ridiculous rules for everything."

Nadine laughed. "I love those people. Is Brother Barnswell still at church playing the mouth organ?"

Tara rolled her eyes. "I knew you would love them and yes, he is still there with the ridiculous thing. Anyway, even though I am usually unhappy to be here, I must say that I am not feeling as bad this weekend.

"By the way, because you told Grandma that Brandon is your guest she said he should stay at the great house with us. She is up there baking bread and doing all sorts of domestic things. I came down here to escape; don't tell her that you saw me."

Nadine laughed and waited at the door while Brandon looked at the various pictures.

"Fascinating," he said, turning to her. "Your family has had this land for close to a century."

"Yes," Nadine nodded. "It's quite a history. You are staying at the great house, and I am sure that Grandpa will tell you some of it."

"No cabin then?" Brandon raised an eyebrow.

"No, my grandparents decided that you are their guest this weekend. Sorry about the peace and quiet thing."

Brandon inhaled appreciatively. "I can already feel the peace. I am looking forward to this weekend."

"Well come on then," Nadine said, holding the door open. "Grandma is cooking. It is sure to be something special. I am suddenly famished."

"Don't tell her where I am," Tara warned when they headed through the door.

*****

The plantation house was on an incline overlooking rolling mountains and acres and acres of green coffee plants.

"It is a good thing I brought my camera," Brandon said when they were standing in the driveway and looking out. "It is gorgeous," he laughed when he felt the cool, almost cold breeze, "and it is a good thing I brought my jacket." He pulled out his two bags.

Nadine looked out over the view and sighed. "I like coming home to the Blue Mountains."

"You aren't cold?" Brandon asked.

"Not really, not yet," Nadine said, "but I will be. It gets really chilly at night."

"Chilly? What an understatement." Brandon shrugged into his jacket and aimed the camera at her. "Smile."

She smiled and he clicked away.

"Oh my," a voice said from the veranda, "Nadine Langley, you are home."

Brandon watched as Nadine and her grandma had an emotional reunion, hugging each other and talking in low, loving tones.

When Nadine finally introduced him as her friend, her

grandmother gave him a thorough once-over and then nodded her head. "Nice to meet you, Brandon Blake. You can call me Nonna. Everybody does." She had a lovely voice. Brandon could imagine her reading children stories by a fire.

He didn't know why that image came to his mind. He was also surprised to note that Nadine looked a bit like her. They had the same hair style except that Nonna's hair was completely white with a purple rinse and she had green eyes—clear, sparkling green eyes...

"Come on in," Nonna said. "I gave Brandon the blue room. Nadine, you sleep in your usual room. The two of you settle down a bit and then come down for dinner."

Nadine showed him to a room that was painted in a pastel blue. It was a large bedroom. Center stage was a four-poster bed with its own curtain tied back to the bed. He had only ever seen beds like this in historical movies.

He sat on it, bouncing a little and feeling like a kid again. It was comfortable and he laid back, looking through the canopy. He could sleep right now, forget about today and his meeting with Ashley. He could forget anything right now he was feeling that comfortable.

He closed his eyes for just a bit. He was jerked awake by a soft touch. Nadine was smiling at him; the side lamps were on.

"I wasn't sure if you had eaten anything today." She sat on the bed beside him. He blinked at the lights and then groaned. "What time is it?"

"Seven o'clock. Nonna did a hearty dinner and she made strawberry pie."

Brandon smiled. "I'd get up just for that. This bed is hypnotic."

Nadine smiled. "Or maybe you are just tired and careworn and need some rest."

Brandon sat up and they stared at each other. The air was heavy with unspoken emotions.

Nadine was the first to look away. "We are going to have family devotion now, and Grandpa wants to meet you."

"Yes." Brandon got up and stretched. He looked at her; the lamp at the side of the bed gave her skin a glow. "You look so beautiful in the half light."

Nadine flushed to the roots of her hair. She knew that her ears were deep red when she backed away from him, as if he insulted her.

"See you downstairs." She stumbled out of the room. Her heart had started its insane rhythmical pounding and she found that she was gasping for breath.

She leaned on the wall when she closed the door. She thought that he looked beautiful in the half-light, and his sleepy eyes made him appear a little vulnerable; he looked yummy as he stretched his lean muscles.

She closed her eyes; she needed to tighten her resolve to not find him so attractive.

*****

It wasn't working for her. They had been browbeaten by Tara to hike to the top of the peak on Sunday morning with her new crush, Gersham, and his church group. Brandon had wanted to go because he had never been to the top of the Blue Mountains, and she had gone along because Brandon was going.

The weekend was going well so far; her grandparents seemed to like him very much. That was no surprise to her; Brandon was an easy guy to like.

She should know her head was higher up in the clouds than it should be. It was four-thirty in the morning and as they climbed along the trail she found herself daydreaming. She imagined that Brandon wasn't married, that he was just a jaded engineer who was tired from his job and was looking for some relaxation in the Blue Mountains, and she had just visited her grandparents and met him in the lounge area of the main cabin.

He turned and looked at her and smiled and instantly. He knew that she was the one for him... She was rudely jerked out of her reverie when one of the guys from the church crew shouted to somebody in the back.

"Watch your step!"

She needed to do the same. She needed to watch her step with Brandon too; no woman in her right mind should be having daydreams about a man whose future was so fluid. It was like hanging a sign around your neck and declaring, *Here I am, hurt me.*

She looked down at the trail and tried hard to concentrate. Was she coveting Brandon?

She didn't think so; it wasn't as if Ashley and he were together. They didn't live together anymore. They were as good as broken up. Well, not really broken up; as Tenaj would say, "A married man is still married until that ink on the divorce paper is dry, Missy." She could even hear Tenaj's voice in its snarky clarity as she walked up hill.

She forced herself not to sigh. She was doing too much of that lately. Why, oh why did she have to fall in love with a married man? She wasn't the type to even consider getting involved in these kinds of situations or think that she would be caught up in one. She remembered how she had blamed Heather for years for dating her father before he was free of her mother. She had looked down her nose at Heather for quite a while.

She had even called her desperate, but here she was in the

same situation. There was no excuse under the sun for having this type of feeling. If only her heart could just cooperate.

They reached the peak a little before the sunrise. It was bitterly cold.

Brandon stood beside her, rubbing his hands. "As difficult as it was getting up here, I would do it again. My feet are going to protest tomorrow."

"Mine too," Nadine said, her lips trembling. "We used to do this a lot when I was younger but living in Kingston has softened me somewhat."

There were only a few of the guys from the group who had also reached the peak, but they were some distance from them.

Brandon turned to her. She could feel his eyes on her face. It was foggy, and the visibility was not all that great. He took her gloved hands in his and then bent his head and kissed her on the lips.

What she had assumed was supposed to be a light kiss deepened into something more when she opened her lips in a gasp. Brandon drew her closer and kissed them apart. From that first instant of contact, Nadine was electrified. Lightning heat sizzled through her.

Her hands came up to clutch at his broad shoulders, and she clung to him. He drew her even closer to him and she surrendered with enthusiasm. As she strained up to him in a fever of desire, with a driven groan, Brandon dragged his mouth from hers and stared down at her with stunned intensity.

The noise from the rest of the hikers made them draw apart and Nadine wrapped her hands around herself as her body hummed with a low intensity of awareness. She felt sensitive everywhere. She wasn't even feeling cold anymore, even though she could see her breath on the air.

When the sun came up, slowly cracking the skies in a pink and orange glow, she looked across at Brandon and realized that he was looking at her too.

"Good morning," he said to her softly.

Nadine laughed. Her breath formed a white smoke in the air. After such an earth-shattering kiss, 'good morning' was the last thing she was expecting.

"Good morning," she smiled. "As Gramps would say, we are flirting with trouble, you know that?"

Brandon nodded. "I know that. I know that better than anybody else."

"Hey, let me take a picture of you guys," Tara said, walking up to them. "You look good together right here."

Brandon handed Tara his camera and he pulled Nadine closer to him as they posed in the new morning on top of the mountain peak.

Chapter Ten

They drove back to Kingston in relative silence after the weekend. Brandon closed his eyes and leaned back in the seat while Nadine drove through the hills.

"Are you sleeping?" she asked softly.

"No." Brandon cracked his eyes open a bit.

"Good, so I can turn on the radio." She did but most of the radio stations were not clear. She pushed in a CD instead. And a Gramps Langley song came on: "It's Torture To Love You."

Nadine started singing along, *It's torture to see you everyday, knowing that you will never come my way ...*

Brandon sat up straighter, more alert, and looked at her.

Nadine glanced at him. "I am going to be doing a cover of it for the Lovers' Rock album the studio is producing. The children and grandchildren of the reggae greats are covering their parents' songs. I chose this one from Gramps and I hadn't even met you yet. Weird, huh?"

Brandon groaned. "Nadine..."

"I know, I know..." Nadine nodded. "You are married; what did I expect? But you kissed me. Well, I participated and I am not going to play coy or beat around the bush. I liked it. I want more than stolen kisses from a married guy but I am finding it difficult to shake you from my mind. Maybe it's a fluke...maybe I don't really like you...maybe I am talking too much."

"Pull over," Brandon said to her softly.

She was getting agitated and she felt like crying so she pulled over on the side of the road and put her head on the steering wheel. "I am stupid."

Brandon cleared his throat and Nadine lifted her head and slowly looked at him.

"No, you are not. I am sorry," Brandon said.

"For what?" Nadine whispered. "It's not your fault that I am acting on the edge of crazy."

Brandon released his seat belt and leaned toward her, wiping a stray tear that had slid down her cheek. "I like you too, Nadine. It's not one-sided. I have been suppressing it. This morning, I shouldn't have kissed you. Nothing in my life is resolved. Kissing you added complication that we don't need."

Nadine turned her cheek into his hand. "I go away in one week, next week Monday."

She raised her head and took a deep breath. "I am going to try and forget you then, I swear. I know I can do it." She laughed. "Maybe I'll find a cute European guy who will make it easier for me to forget."

Brandon frowned. "I don't think I like the sound of that."

"Well, too bad, Mister," Nadine said determinedly. "I am Nadine Langley. I am a gorgeous and talented woman, and I can find myself my own single guy."

Brandon looked at her worriedly. "I hate the idea of you finding a guy."

"Why?" Nadine looked at him hopefully. "You feel jealous?"

"Like crazy," Brandon said, inhaling roughly when he realized what he admitted.

He kept glancing at her all the way to Kingston. It was amazing how jealous he felt at just the thought of her being with somebody else. It made him uneasy. It felt worse than having caught Ashley cheating, and that was saying a lot because that night he had felt gutted.

He pondered that for a while. When had he gotten over seeing Ashley with Regina? He didn't feel as thunderously angry when he thought about it. He didn't feel anything at all. Especially not for Ashley. What he felt now was a feeling of passivity. Maybe he should get the divorce ball rolling.

*****

Monday morning Brandon got up with aching limbs. It was a wakeup call for him; he hadn't been exercising for months. He always took his slim frame for granted but obviously the Blue Mountain experience was showing him up.

He contemplated pulling on his sweats and walking up and down the Smoky Vale hills several times. He could put in a half an hour and then come back home to get ready for work. When he drove down to the foot of the hill he saw groups of people doing the same thing.

He was pleasantly surprised to find that most walkers were very pleasant. He said good morning several times to sweaty-faced persons in sleeveless shirts, while he shivered in his sweatshirt, pushing his hands in his pocket for warmth.

"Brandon Blake!" He spun around and he saw a short

portly man holding a dumbbell heading toward him with a smile on his bearded face.

"Pastor Wiggan!" Brandon beamed. "I didn't know you lived up here."

"Yes, I do now," Pastor Wiggan said, drawing level with him. "I didn't know you lived up here either. Small world, eh? Walking alone without Ashley. Too early for her, huh?"

Brandon grimaced and didn't answer. "You know, I was thinking of you the other day, how you told me not to marry Ashley. That was pretty prophetic. Ashley and I are on the outs. She still lives in Norbrook. I am just crashing here for the time being."

"Oh," Pastor Wiggan nodded. "That was eight or so years ago, wasn't it? I have since repented of saying that. I always felt a little bad about pulling you aside and telling you that you should reconsider. Your marriage, I thought, lasted much longer than some of the more compatible couples I have counseled. Is there any hope of reconciliation?"

"I don't think so." Brandon sighed. "I am tired of working on it and now when Ashley claims that she wants to, my enthusiasm is gone."

"That's too bad," Pastor Wiggan said, breathing heavily as they picked up speed walking down the hill. "Have you prayed about it?"

"Every night," Brandon said, "but I think I am hampered by the fact that I have feelings for someone else. I really don't want to work on my half-dead marriage anymore. I am ready to move on."

"Good Lord," Pastor Wiggan whispered. "We had a marriage conference the other day, where psychiatrists and counselors come together and talk about their profession, and you know what they found? When either party in a marriage forms new emotional attachments with others, the marriage is as good as dead."

Brandon snorted. "Through the years my marriage has teetered on the brink of collapse. I stayed because of the kids, but when I caught Ashley cheating I think that was a wakeup call."

"She cheated?" the pastor panted, slowing down as they came to the bottom of the hill.

"Yes, and that was just icing on the cake," Brandon scowled. "We have been having problems for years; if I say left, Ashley says right."

Pastor Wiggan was silent when they walked back up the hill. When they neared the middle he panted, "Brandon, you know the Bible says it is only through the hardness of our hearts why we get divorced."

Brandon stopped beside him. "I hear you."

"Give your marriage a working chance, Brandon," Pastor Wiggan said, wheezing. "Put aside the new relationship for now and give your marriage a chance—I am so out of shape it is not funny."

Brandon glanced at his watch. "I have to leave now. I have to go to Norbrook to get the kids ready."

"You have to do that?" Pastor Wiggan asked, frowning. "Isn't Ashley there?"

"It's my job to do it." Brandon waved to him and prepared to run up the hill. "I am quite happy to do it, actually."

"Remember what I said," Pastor Wiggan called after him. "Give your marriage a chance."

*****

"Brandon, we need to talk about Christmas," Ashley greeted him at the door. "The kids' vacation will begin Wednesday. Alisha has a part in some Christmas play today-- did you know about that?—and Ariel is supposed to be an angel at her school. I can't deal with this! I have a store to run. This is my busiest period."

"Good morning to you too," Brandon said, glancing at her. She was dressed to the nines in an all-red suit and her signature killer heels. "I have never seen you up this early, and yes I knew about the play; it's up on the activity board."

Ashley snorted. "I don't have time for activity boards. I have a buyer at seven. Some important millionaire guy with his mistress. I have to be the one who personally meets them. I want to know if these people sleep. Seven in the morning is an unholy time to shop but then again, the girl is his mistress, so they probably have to sneak around."

She headed to the kitchen.

"So how was your weekend with the kids and your mom?"

"Horrible," Ashley threw over her shoulders. "So horrible my mother actually accused me of not being a good mother. Isn't that like the pot calling the kettle black? She was never there for me in my childhood, so of course we argued about that, and then Ariel was acting like a brat. She wouldn't keep still, bawling and moping around the place. When I told her to stop it she cried like a banshee, like I was abusing her or something. Last night she didn't sleep. I tried calling you yesterday; where were you?"

"The Blue Mountains," Brandon grinned. "I had a peaceful time."

"My kids, my own kids are a nightmare with me," Ashley said raggedly, putting the kettle on. "Why? It's as if the little monsters want to show me up."

"Where are they?" Brandon asked. "You didn't just leave them to get ready, did you?"

"Yes," Ashley gritted out. "Alisha is seven. She is not a baby any more. She should be able to see to her and Ariel.

Those children are too dependent. You are hampering their development with your constant helpfulness."

Brandon stared at her, speechless. He didn't know what to say. Did it even make sense to argue that children need a helpful and guiding hand when they were at the girls' ages? He spun around and left her.

"Since you are here, I guess I can leave them into your capable hands." Ashley shouted at his retreating back. "And I can't make it to the play. I already told Alisha. I know you'll be going so please take pictures or a video or something."

When Brandon went to the children's room they were fast asleep, as he knew they would be. Ashley probably just came to the door and woke them up, not waiting to see if they were up.

*****

"Mom, I am swamped." Brandon was at his desk, trying to leave the office by one. He was clearing out his desk. Today was technically his last day at work. Alisha had a play, and Ariel had a play an hour after that. He had to be calling in the family for backup.

"I can't make it, Brandon," his mother said like she was rushing. "Your father and I are helping out at the main bakery today. We promised Latoya."

"Okay," he said and hung up. He could go to Alisha's play and then take the back roads to reach Ariel's school in time for her play.

She was going to be an angel with one line. She had been practicing all morning: "Peace on earth and goodwill to men." If he didn't make it he would be in serious trouble.

He was on his way out of the office when Nadine called.

"Hey," she said sweetly. "I am free for the afternoon; want

to come see my studio and meet Gramps Langley?"

"Ah Nadine," Brandon said, "I wish I could but I have two school plays to go to."

"Oh," Nadine said, "I haven't been to a school play since I was in school." She chuckled. "You and Ashley splitting time?"

"No. Actually, Ashley is not coming," Brandon said, grabbing his car keys. "You want to come? We could all go up to your studio after."

"Sure," Nadine said, "it should be fun. I get to meet your girls."

"You are crazy...mad...mentally unhinged," Tenaj said when Nadine hung up the phone.

"Thanks," Nadine said, grabbing her handbag.

"Not a compliment," Tenaj said disapprovingly. "Just a few days ago you said you were going to stop seeing Brandon Blake; today you are going to his kid's play."

"I know," Nadine said. "I just like him, okay?"

Tenaj snorted. "This looks more than like to me, young one."

"You are just three years older than me," Nadine laughed. "Do you think that this outfit is appropriate for a school play?"

"No," Tenaj said, shaking her head vigorously. "Khaki three-quarter pants and red shirt, not appropriate, especially when the school play involves Ashley Blake's children."

"For heaven's sake." Nadine walked to the office door. "Brandon said he'd come back here with me. When he does, can you play nice?"

Tenaj beamed. "I can play nice."

"Don't lecture him on the sanctity of marriage or anything like that," Nadine said anxiously. "He's just a friend. Please remember."

Tenaj nodded. "Just a friend that you spent a weekend with in the Blue Mountains and carry to your studio and meet his kids. Yes, I understand."

"That's what friends do." Nadine rolled her eyes. "Be nice when I get back here."

*****

Nadine found St. Michael's Prep School for girls quite easily; that was where Brandon said she should meet him first. The car park was crowded but she found a parking space and then rushed to the entrance of the auditorium. She looked around for Brandon. He was sitting near a window seat; he waved her over when he spotted her.

She sat beside him. "Hey. Did I miss anything?"

Brandon squeezed her hand and she felt the familiar tingle when he was near.

"No," he whispered. "My girl is the lead singer in a song for the musical. There's her name." He pointed to the Alisha Blake that was printed on the program with pride. "This play should last for just a half hour; all else being equal, I can then rush over to Ariel's play."

Nadine smiled at him. "You are such a good dad." *And a handsome man.* He was in a white shirt, the two top buttons undone. His face was cleanly shaven and he smelled good. A few of the mothers in the audience were checking him out. One in particular kept craning her head in his direction. When she saw Nadine her mouth turned down in a disappointed moue. Of course, Brandon saw none of this; he was probably unaware of the kind of stir his presence caused. He was sitting in the auditorium along with just a handful of men, and he was by far the most handsome guy there. The single mothers and maybe some of the married mothers must be having a field day checking him out.

Nadine sympathized with the disappointed lady. *It's you and me, lady. I really have no right to be by his side either.*

"You think so?" Brandon whispered. "Lately I have been worrying that I am not all that."

Nadine grinned. "You are all that. Seriously!"

Before she could say anything else the program began. Nadine descended into fantasy land again. She imagined that she was there with Brandon, Alisha was their child, and she was attending the musical to support her.

She was snapped out of her reverie when Brandon got up. "I have to get a better angle to tape this," he said, moving to the end of the aisle. She's up next."

When the performance was over and Alisha and her group got a standing ovation, Brandon came back and breathed a sigh of relief. "I was so nervous." He looked at Nadine ruefully. "I know, I am a clichéd overprotective parent."

Nadine smiled. She hoped that the love that she was feeling for him wasn't shining from her eyes. Nothing on this planet was sexier than a father who loved his children.

"You are not a cliché, trust me. My dad loves me to death but the truth is, like probably ninety percent of the children here, Daddy couldn't make it to these sort of things back when I was in prep school, but when he did, oh my, it was the greatest thing. Your girls are super lucky."

*****

When the play was finished, Brandon headed to the front of the auditorium. Nadine followed him at a sedate pace.

"Oh Mr. Blake, you made it," Miss Jackson, a bespectacled lady in a long dress said while shaking his hand.

"I wouldn't miss it." Brandon smiled. He hugged Alisha to

him. "You did great, honey."

"Thank you, Daddy." Alisha was bubbling over with excitement at her latest accomplishment. It made Nadine smile.

"Mrs. Blake," Miss Jackson said, turning to Nadine. "I am so happy to finally meet you. "

Brandon looked at Nadine and raised his brow.

Nadine flushed. She was not Mrs. Blake but she liked how it sounded. She cleared her throat. "No, I am not Mrs. Blake. I am Nadine, Brandon's friend. I was just here to give support."

"Oh." Mrs. Jackson adjusted her glasses on her nose. "Yes, of course. Nadine Langley. How awkward. I am sorry. I didn't recognize you at first. I love your gospel song, 'Blessings'. I am going to teach it to my homeroom next year."

"That's a great compliment." Nadine nodded.

"We have to go," Brandon said to Mrs. Jackson. "I have another play in ten minutes."

"Okay then," Mrs. Jackson smiled, "all the best to little Miss Ariel."

*****

Nadine followed Brandon after the little exchange, feeling ridiculously happy. When she had her own children she would probably relish these little things too: school plays, PTA meetings and the whole works. Even if she didn't have her own, she had no problems coming to Alisha's and Ariel's events. It would be an honor. If she was the next Mrs. Blake, she would be the best stepmother she could be to his girls.

She squashed the niggling voice that told her that she was building castles in the sky. It would only result in pain. She could see it now: Ashley would reclaim her husband and she would be hurt. And when had she moved from loving Brandon to wanting to marry him. She was well and truly smitten. Wasn't there a long timeline for this kind of thing?

She wasn't sure; she had never loved a guy before, or felt this strong sort of chemical imbalance. The jury was still out on her current emotions.

After Ariel's play, Brandon took the girls to Devon House for ice cream, and Nadine followed.

"Hi again," Nadine said as the girls licked their ice cream under a gazebo.

"Hi," Brandon smiled at her. "Girls this is Nadine."

Nadine looked at his two girls and smiled. They looked nothing like Brandon or Ashley. She had noticed this at both of their school plays.

Alisha smiled at her shyly, and Ariel was effervescent. She came around to where Nadine sat and started chattering. She opened her arms in a wide gesture. "Peace on earth, and goodwill to men."

"She is not going to stop saying it," Brandon chuckled. He reached for a wet napkin and wiped Ariel's dress front where the ice cream spilled.

"Your dress is pretty," Nadine said to Ariel. She was in a frilly white dress. After all, she had been an angel.

"Thank you," Ariel beamed.

They were surprisingly well behaved and easy to talk to, Nadine found out. She had to take Ariel to the bathroom, and she felt like a real, honest-to-goodness mom while she cleaned her up and helped her back into her clothes.

"Your daughter is pretty," a lady said to her in the wash room. "How old is she?"

"Three," Nadine said, once again feeing like a proud mom. The feeling was completely inappropriate.

"Your guy is white, huh?" The lady asked.

Nadine, in the midst of washing her hands, stared at her, appalled. "No, he's not."

"She looks a lot like my daughter Brianna and she's biracial too. This whole genes thing is amazing, though." The lady laughed and left the washroom.

Nadine dried her hand and took Ariel's hand and they walked out of the washroom.

"Why is the sun yellow?" Ariel asked her as she tried to skip into the patches of sunshine on the paved walk.

Nadine chuckled. She didn't know what to answer. Before she could formulate a response in her head, Ariel was asking her another question and skipping along merrily. Nadine realized that she could get away by not answering anything too difficult.

She was looking at Ariel's happy sunny face and wondering about her genes. The lady in the bathroom was being ridiculous.

Nadine's eyes were hazel, and she had wavy hair. She got that from her mother's side of the family. Her mom had dark brown eyes. Tara had dark brown eyes and her aunt May had green eyes like her mother's.

Ariel must have gotten her very light complexion and light brown eyes from somewhere in either Brandon's or Ashley's family tree. Genes were really tricky.

When she joined Brandon and Alisha, she had answered a ton of questions from Ariel, who didn't want to release her fingers.

Brandon watched their linked fingers with a smile on his face.

"I have never seen Ariel take to anyone in so short a time," he whispered to Nadine. "You know what they say about children and animals sniffing out the good in people."

Nadine laughed. "Children sniffing, really?"

Brandon grinned. "Figure of speech...Good people are like a magnet for children. They instinctively know when someone is good. I guess God made us all with that level of discernment and we lose it the older we get.

""Girls, want to see what a recording studio looks like?" Brandon asked them.

"Yes!" Alisha's eyes were shining. "When I grow up I want to be a singer."

*****

The girls were a big hit at the studio. Gramps was in his element as he did a duet with Alisha, who was sitting beside him, intently watching his fingers on the guitar strings.

Ariel followed Nadine and climbed into her lap when she sat down.

Tenaj raised her brows and started laughing when Ariel curled her hand around Nadine's neck and promptly fell asleep.

"Big day for her," Nadine whispered lovingly.

"It suits you," Tenaj said, "the whole motherhood thing. You have always had that soft touch and I know now why you like Brandon so much," she whispered. "He's lovely. Fine as hell. Girl..."

"No lectures," Nadine hissed. "Now is not the time."

Brandon came to the office door and looked over at Nadine. "She's sleeping? I am going to have to take them home now. Nice meeting you, Tenaj."

"Same here," Tenaj smiled. "Your girls are lovely. Say hi to Ashley for me; I know her pretty well.

Brandon nodded. "I can't promise that I will relay the message. This is a busy time of the year for her. She probably won't be at home."

He took Ariel from Nadine and mouthed, "Thanks. I'll call you."

When they were walking out with Nadine behind them, Alisha asked shyly, "Nadine, would you like to come to the end of year Thanksgiving service at my church? I'll be singing."

Nadine looked over at Brandon and then at Alisha. "Sure, thanks for inviting me. I will be back from tour then. A day before."

"Okay," Alisha said happily. "Have a great tour."

"Thank you," Nadine said softly.

"Such a polite girl," Gramps said when they stood at the door and watched as Brandon drove through the studio gates.

"And a handsome married father," Tenaj said wistfully.

"Oh shut up," Nadine growled.

"Do you think you should be going to their end-of-year thing?" Tenaj asked. "Nadine, you are in over your head. Your eyes light up when the man is around, and you are looking on his children as if they are yours."

"Yes, I am going to the thing at the end of the year. It's at their church; I would have gone to my church in any case." She chose to ignore the rest of Tenaj's rant. "I am fine."

"What about your resolve to get Brandon out of your head?" Tenaj folded her arms and looked at her sternly.

"You've seen him," Nadine said weakly. "You've talked to him. You know what he is like now. Please give me a Brandon antidote and I'll take it."

Tenaj sighed. "Yes, I have to admit he is different, but girl...I am no prophetess, but I think any woman in her right mind will come to her senses and snatch back that man. As far as I know, Ashley is in her right mind."

Chapter Eleven

Brandon turned off the night-light and closed the door as soon as the children fell asleep. Juliet had called in sick with the flu and he had to wait until Ashley got home.

He went to his home office and looked around. He hadn't been in there for so long that his stuff had started gathering dust. He glanced through a stack of files that he had downloaded and printed regarding Canada and Harold's business.

He sat down in his squeaking chair and looked over the information. He had been seriously contemplating making the move a year ago to get a fresh start. He massaged his nose bridge. He couldn't move now. He had the girls to think of, and uprooting them from school would not be good. He had to decide about what to do about his failed relationship with Ashley, and he would be moving away from the start of something new and, he hoped, better with Nadine.

He picked up the phone. He was going to check out Harold's

offer of doing a three-month stint with him in the New Year. That was a long enough time for him to decide. He could take January to sort out things here and go in February.

"There you are." Ashley leaned on the doorjamb. "Where's Juliet?"

"Sick." Brandon looked at her with some surprise. She looked tired and slightly off kilter, like some of the stuffing had gone out of her. "She said she called you yesterday evening."

Ashley sat across from him in an inelegant heap, "I barely heard her at the time. I was so busy with a million and one things on my brain. I hope the girls don't get sick too. I couldn't handle that along with this crazy season."

Brandon nodded and then said after an awkward silence, "The plays were good. Alisha sang her piece without a mistake and Ariel got her line right."

Ashley smiled. "I am happy. I feel like a deadbeat mom. I am so sorry that I couldn't make it. Today was super busy. I have been on my feet nonstop all day."

"There'll be more plays," Brandon said helpfully. "Try to go to at least some of them."

Ashley massaged her temples. "Well, thank God for technology; you did record a video, didn't you?"

"Yes, I did." Brandon searched his bag for his camera and took out the card. "Please return it to me." He handed it to her. "I haven't taken off any of the photos yet."

"Thanks." Ashley took out the pins out of her chignon one by one and then breathed a sigh of relief as her hair cascaded down her shoulders.

"So, where are you going to spend Christmas?"

"With my parents," Brandon said, "as I do every year. The last couple of years you conveniently never showed up."

"I can barely wake up on Christmas Day after the Christmas

Eve rush on the store," Ashley murmured. "I am sure you and your family understand that."

"Yes." Brandon nodded. "I do. I am not sure about my family. But you don't have any Christmas memories with your children. Maybe it's time you start thinking of creating some, especially since you can."

"Let's not argue." Ashley growled. "I think it is well established that I am not a traditional mother, not like yours. But I still love my children. Why do I have to keep defending myself to everybody?"

Brandon looked at her mutely. In the past, this was where he would flare up and point out all her shortcomings and then that would be the start of a fight that would segue into a cold war that lasted days, until he apologized, because Ashley never apologized for anything. He was the one who was always in the wrong.

He got up. "Well, see you."

"What do you mean by 'see you'?" Ashley's lips trembled. "Can't you just stay? They don't have school tomorrow and I have to go to the store early."

"Okay," Brandon said, "I'll stay. Tomorrow I have to go clear out my office. Technically it is my last day there."

"And then what?" Ashley rubbed her scalp rhythmically.

"Then I take a month's vacation in January, finish up some private projects and then head to Canada for three months."

"Oh no, Brandon, you can't leave for that long." Ashley stopped rubbing her scalp and turned to him.

"Why?" Brandon asked cynically. "You'll miss me?"

"I am not a single parent, nor do I want to be," Ashley said roughly. "The girls can't go with you, can they? So they'll be left with me."

"I have never before seen anyone so afraid of parenting their own children," Brandon snarled. "Suck it up, Ashley.

Maybe then you can try to bond with them. You need to make more of an effort."

"That's unfair," Ashley snapped, "so unfair. I do my share of parenting. I changed diapers when they were younger and did the whole staying up late thing. I am not going to let you imply otherwise."

"Whatever." Brandon headed for the guest room, which was across from the girls' room. "I was there, I don't need to argue about what you did or did not do. And I can tell you that you didn't do anything much."

"Aren't you going to sleep in our bed?" Ashley walked behind him.

"No," Brandon said abruptly. "I am working on getting the image of you and Regina in the bed out of my head. It's not happening. I may never sleep in that bed again."

He closed the door in her face before she could protest.

*****

Ashley made a face at the door. She hated how Brandon was making her out to be the villain. Apart from her little indiscretions, she was a good person, she reasoned to herself. She wasn't a bad mother. So what if she wasn't a Beatrice Blake? She had her own style of parenting. Making cookies and playing with them wasn't her style, but she loved her kids.

She went and looked in on them, tucking the sheet under Ariel and kissing her gently on the cheek and putting Alisha's teddy bear closer to her.

She left the room and paused as she looked at Brandon's door. She wished he could be swayed with sex. They could be reconciled by the morning. She would pull out all the seductive stops, but she knew Brandon well. She knew what that withering look just now meant: *Stay away; I don't want you.*

She headed to her room to watch the children's school play before going to bed. She would make an effort as Brandon said, prove to him that she was changing, win him back. She wanted back the husband that would do anything for her. She wanted what she had before.

The month apart taught her what she said earlier; she was not great at doing the single parent thing. She had to convince Brandon that he shouldn't leave.

It was ironic; a few weeks ago she was talking divorce, but now the thought scared her. She had no doubt that she could find somebody else soon, but nobody else was quite like Brandon. You never miss the water till the well runs dry. Now, she understood what that meant.

She showered and put on her negligee and grabbed her laptop, putting the photo card in the drive.

She glanced idly at the file called Blue Mountain. She had no idea why Brandon found nature so interesting. He took pictures of misty mountains and flowers and strawberries. She paused when she saw a picture of Nadine Langley, and then another and another and then one with Brandon standing beside her, with the mountain serving as a backdrop.

Ashley bit her tongue and then maximized the photo and looked at their smiling features. He had his hand around Nadine. He looked happy and relaxed. She had not seen Brandon looking like this for years, not since their honeymoon.

She gasped. Brandon Blake, her super husband, was having an affair with Nadine Langley? No, Brandon was not the type of guy to have affairs. When had he even met Nadine?

She got up from the bed. She was steaming mad. She wanted to go and knock on the guest room door and demand that he explain. She wanted to smash something. How dare Brandon act like he was better than her because he caught her with Regina, when all along he was happy with someone else?

She couldn't sleep now; she didn't even look at the video of the girls. She stormed toward the door and flung it open. When she pounded on the guest room door four times, he opened it sleepily.

"Ashley, what's all the noise for?"

"Are you having an affair with Nadine Langley?" she growled.

Brandon paused. "What gave you that idea?"

"I saw pictures of the two of you in Blue Mountains. You looked happy," she finished accusingly. "Happier than I have seen you in years."

Brandon mused. "That's quite telling, isn't it? I am happy when I am around Nadine. She is uncomplicated and has a lovely personality and is drama free. There is a lot to be said about a drama-free life."

"So you are having an affair!" Ashley screeched.

"Keep your voice down," Brandon whispered. "No, I am not having an affair. Now go to bed."

Ashley looked at him accusingly. "You are no better than me."

Brandon laughed briefly. "I would say something mean to counteract that, but never mind. Goodnight, Ashley."

He closed the door in her face again; this time she kicked it.

*****

When Ashley came downstairs in the morning she felt woozy and sleep deprived. She had tossed and turned all night, completely aware now that she really had to fight for her marriage. She had competition for her husband from Nadine Langley.

She believed that he hadn't had an affair yet but when she heard how Brandon spoke fondly about Nadine she knew that it was time that she upped her game. She couldn't play a complacent wait-and-see game anymore. She couldn't wait for Brandon to see sense and come back home.

She was going to have to put more of an effort in getting him back. She was going to have an uphill battle convincing him to forgive her about the incident that he saw with Regina. She was going to have to do a hundred and eighty degree turn. She had won Brandon before, and back then he had posed somewhat of a bigger challenge.

Now she knew what made him tick. She also had something that Nadine didn't have. She had his children, and Brandon loved his children. Nadine Langley might not know it but she was at war with Ashley Blake and Ashley Blake did not like losing.

She had set the alarm to wake her up at six, one hour earlier than her usual time. She forced herself to get ready though she felt sleepy and woke up the girls and got them ready. She dressed them in color-coordinated clothes and had put Ariel's hair in a nice, complicated style.

Ariel had cooperated with her for once and had even hugged her this morning. The kitchen was a scene of domestic bliss when Brandon came down the stairs.

He did a double take when he saw Ashley around the nook eating with the children.

Ashley smiled at him smugly. "I am making an effort."

"So I see." Brandon kissed the girls.

"Daddy, can we go to Nadine's studio today?" Alisha asked. "Gramps said I can come back anytime I want."

Ashley looked at Brandon sharply. "Nadine's studio? They met Gramps Langley?"

"Nadine is nice," Ariel said, clapping her hands. "I like Nadine."

Brandon grinned. "I doubt that today will be a good day to visit Nadine. She is in the final stages of preparing for her tour."

"What's a tour?" Ariel asked.

Ashley glared at Brandon. *So this relationship with Nadine is more involved than I thought. He is taking our children to visit Nadine at her studio.*

"Just how involved are you with Nadine, dear?" Ashley asked sweetly.

Brandon raised his eyebrow at her. "Not as involved as you are with Regina."

"Were," Ashley corrected him. "Were. Past tense. I have put Regina and the whole incident behind me. I am repentant. I wish you would forget it and move on."

Brandon sighed and ignored Ashley. He turned to Ariel. "A tour is like a trip. Nadine will go to several different places and sing."

"Cool." Alisha's eyes widened. "I wish I could do that."

"You are not responding to me," Ashley butted in. "I want us to work, Brandon. I want to be a family again."

"Please Ashley, not in front of the children." Brandon turned to the fridge. "Can't we even agree not to argue in front of the children?"

Ashley got up and stood behind him. "I don't want us to argue. I want us to be on the same page again. I want us to work."

Brandon shrugged. "That would be a minor miracle. You are not a family kind of girl, Ashley. As for being on the same page, I don't even know if we are in the same book."

*****

Brandon took the kids for their vacation leading up to Christmas Day. He had finally cleared up all the loose ends at the office and had set up a small Christmas tree in the apartment that the kids had fun decorating.

On Christmas morning they headed to his parents' place to spend the day with his family. It was the usual fun-filled day that everybody participated in mainly because of the children.

Latoya and his mom spent the earlier part of the day in the kitchen. It was the women's turn in the kitchen. Last year the men had done the catering and it had been an exceptional spread. Latoya and his mom were trying to outdo them this year.

His father was in the basement entertaining the children with a few of his new creations. Brandon and Richard fiddled with the radio in his father's classic Aston Martin. They finally got the radio to work and sat in the car under a mango tree in the leafy shade.

They turned on the radio and leaned back in their seats. Christmas carol after Christmas carol wafted on the air.

"I heard about Ashley," Richard said.

Brandon nodded. "I know Latoya would have reported."

"How are you doing it?" Richard asked. "You are a stronger man than me, you know that? If I had caught my wife with another person, I'd be raging mad. I would probably end up in a mental institution by now. If I had caught her with another woman I'd probably be in the morgue. Along with her and the woman."

"It is what it is. It's amazing the things we can endure when life dishes it out." Brandon bopped his head to a reggae version of the Christmas carol, "Chestnuts Roasting on an Open Fire".

"I am doing better. Much better than when I just found out. That's Gramps Langley," he said in the middle of the song. Instantly he thought of Nadine, not that she was far from his mind. She had called him last night. She said it was cold, colder than the Blue Mountains. They had talked for a while.

"I know." Richard smiled. "Breadfruit roasting on an open fire..."

They laughed together.

Last year they had roasted breadfruit as a part of Christmas lunch.

"Seriously, though, what are you going to do?" Richard asked. "I mean, I know that Latoya told you about Kenneth, my cousin the lawyer."

"I don't know," Brandon said. "If we didn't have the children I would divorce Ashley in a heartbeat."

"But you have the kids," Richard sighed.

"But I have the kids," Brandon repeated and was almost stunned when he saw Ashley's car drive up into the yard.

It was eleven o'clock in the morning. She hadn't visited the house for Christmas since Ariel was born, almost five years ago.

"Oh my," Richard whispered. They both watched as she got out of the car in a stylish yet simple striped dress. Even from where they sat they could see that she was not in her usual war paint. She had her hair pulled back in a ponytail. She looked young and fresh and so much like the Ashley of old that Brandon actually sat up straighter in his seat.

"She is not wearing heels." Richard whispered to Brandon.

"So I see." Brandon watched as she went into the house with several brightly wrapped packages.

Richard grasped the door handle. "Sorry Brandon, I have

to go see this live and in living color. I might have to act as referee if Latoya decides to have a showdown."

Brandon scrambled out of the car too. "I am coming with you."

*****

Ashley could feel the animosity as soon as she entered the kitchen. Latoya had been chopping onions, chef style, her knife flying through the onions, and Beatrice had been stirring something in a pot. When she greeted them, they both had acted as if they saw a ghost. All action had frozen in the kitchen.

She had deliberately avoided Beatrice, her only champion in the Blake family for the past couple of weeks, since Brandon caught her cheating. Predictably, Beatrice was looking at her with disappointment.

Latoya was looking at her with something akin to hatred. The stare was so malevolent that Ashley felt so dirty and small and guilty that she had to force herself to stand there while they looked at her.

What did she expect, absolution? A hearty welcome? She had hurt their son and brother.

Beatrice was the first to speak, a hurt tremor in her voice. "Ashley."

Ashley inclined her head. "Beatrice."

Latoya glared at her and continued chopping the onion with a renewed aggression that made Ashley step back involuntarily. She had no doubt that Latoya was imagining that her neck was the onion.

"I am sorry," she blurted out, "for all the stuff that I did. I am sorry for withdrawing myself from the family. I know I did wrong but I am trying by God's grace to rectify my wrongs."

"You are a two-timing whore," Latoya said snidely. "W-H-O-R-E."

"Latoya!" Beatrice snapped, looking at her daughter with eyes widened with shock.

"Somebody needs to give you a beat down," Latoya snarled. "A thorough beating. You have hung my brother out to dry for years. Years! You should take your apology and shove it."

Beatrice wiped her hand on her apron and put her hand akimbo. "Latoya Blake Cameron, that is not how we treat a person who asks us for forgiveness, and Ashley, you must admit that what you did to Brandon was devastating and you have been avoiding us for a long while.

"However, today is not the day to dwell on this. You are here now. It's the women's turn to cook Christmas dinner. The gungo peas and rice are almost finished. Latoya is doing the honey roasted chicken. You can sweeten the sorrel."

Ashley moved farther into the kitchen.

When she looked behind her she saw Brandon and Richard standing like they were expecting an explosion.

"Can we sit in?" Richard asked eagerly.

"No," Beatrice said, "it's girls' time. You two, out!"

When the guys moved away Beatrice handed Ashley a spoon and a bowl of sugar. "You can also set the table. The stuff is in the side cupboard."

"I remember," Ashley said softly.

Latoya snorted, "It's a miracle she remembers. Why couldn't she have remembered the little word commitment or even loyalty or even heterosexuality or even..."

"Stop Latoya!" Beatrice said. "Cut her some slack."

Latoya harrumphed.

"She's here. It's Christmas. It's family time."

Latoya cut her eyes at Ashley and murmured. "Don't you

come near me, you two-timing hussy. If forgiveness is what you want from this side of the kitchen, please remember that I am not a pushover like my mom or my brother, and I am not being a hypocrite and greeting you with open arms."

Ashley swallowed. "Okay then."

*****

Despite the hostility from Latoya, the rest of the family treated her with politeness. The dinner went smoothly, except for when Alisha started talking about Nadine.

"Is Nadine her new celebrity crush?" Latoya asked, grinning.

Brandon smiled. "I guess so."

"She's coming to our church to ring in the New Year," Alisha said excitedly. "I can't wait."

Ashley stiffened. "Is that so?" She looked at Brandon and raised her brow.

Brandon nodded.

"Did you all know that Brandon is seeing Nadine Langley?" Ashley asked the table in general.

Everybody looked at Brandon.

"She's a friend," Brandon shrugged, "and I like her very much."

"Good for you," Latoya said, pleased. "I am sure she is a vast improvement on the previous female in your life, who you caught cheating with her friend."

Richard started chuckling and then Leonard. Beatrice and Brandon were the only ones who were not laughing.

"We have little ears among us," Beatrice said quietly. "Latoya, you are acting as if you have never committed a sin in your life."

"She is the one who brought it up," Latoya defended.

"Surely she didn't expect us to sympathize with her against Brandon, not after what she did?"

Ashley pushed her food around her plate and then finally looked up with tears in her eyes. "Yes, I am a sinner. Yes, I did wrong but I am working on righting my mistakes and mocking me will not stop me. I love Brandon and I want him back!" She sniffed and got up. "Excuse me."

"Crocodile tears," Latoya called after her. "And if you loved Brandon you wouldn't have..."

"Stop it!" Beatrice chided. "She is trying."

"I don't buy it," Latoya pointed her fork at Brandon, "and neither should you."

Brandon looked at Alisha, who had hung her head over her plate. He pointed to her and Latoya nodded.

"Okay, I'll behave myself now."

Brandon was happy when they moved on to happier topics. When Ashley returned to the table they even included her in their conversations for the kids' sake.

He wondered if that was what he was going to have to do too—stay with Ashley for their sake.

Chapter Twelve

Ashley hung up the phone from her counselor and sat down on the settee. She had booked another day in the week for counseling. God, she needed the help.

She stared at a picture that was on the mantle in front of her: she and Brandon on board a cruise ship. She was grinning and Brandon was solemn, looking at her contemplatively. She had always liked the picture because she looked good in it. Her shape had bounced back after Alisha and she had been in a yellow string bikini that showed how good she looked, but now that she observed the picture closely, she looked like the only one having fun.

Brandon looked miserable and unhappy, like his hand was around her but he wasn't really there. Like he wished he was somewhere else. It was a far cry from that picture that he had taken with Nadine on the Blue Mountains that was for sure. She hated that dratted picture but the image of Brandon smiling and relaxed was stuck in her head and she couldn't shake it.

The cruise had been a second honeymoon—the second year of their marriage, after her affair with Carlos and the birth of Alisha. She had wanted a fresh start and Brandon had, as always, been willing to try and make things work. They had fought for months before that. Simple things, like who closed the front door or who turned on the light in the kitchen and left it on.

She closed her eyes in defeat. He wasn't willing to try anything now. He was as aloof and cold as she had ever seen him. After the hazardous Christmas dinner with the Blake family that she had psyched herself for, ate humble pie and attended, Brandon didn't even seem impressed that she had made an effort. He had shunned her for the week that followed.

He had taken the kids, and he was away with his sister and her husband, enjoying the holiday, light-hearted and free. The last time she called him they had gone fishing. They were having some grand adventure as a family without her. She was never involved and never wanted to be, but now that she was on the outs with Brandon she desperately wanted to be included in their family fun.

She realized that as far as the children's affections went, she would be second best to Brandon. To make the effort now would invite more ridicule; besides, she didn't want to be anywhere near Latoya. The woman actively detested her.

The thought made her feel lonelier than ever. She had never felt so out of it before. Usually she had something to occupy her thoughts. If it wasn't an affair, it was business and now with nothing but the clock ticking away and the new year approaching she felt a loneliness so severe, she was even tempted to call Regina.

Regina, who she had cut out of her life like a cankerous

sore. Regina had laughed with confidence and told her that she would need her again.

She tightened her hands against the satiny cushion and a few tears slipped down her cheeks. The counselor had told her in the last session that she shouldn't wallow in self-pity, that everybody made mistakes, and all she needed to do was pick herself up and do better again.

It was easier said than done. She had never really been the humble type; she was always scheming, always trying to win.

When she realized early in her marriage that she wouldn't be able to keep up her perfect wife façade, she had given up and had an affair; when she had realized early in motherhood that the baby seemed more bonded to Brandon, she had given up and let him just handle everything. When she had realized early in her Christian walk that she could not keep up with the seemingly dedicated Christian folk, she had also given up.

Ashley Blake was not a fighter. She loved competition but only if she was sure of a win, and that was why she was in the half dark on New Year's Eve, friendless, husbandless and family-less. She had given up.

Her therapist said she had a personality disorder and that it wasn't impossible to fix it, but right now, under the pressing weight of all that she had done, she didn't know if she could ever be fixed and even if she could, she would not have Brandon again; she had lost.

Just then the clock struck five-thirty and she remembered that there was a program at the church and Nadine was going to be there to see Alisha sing. She realized that the fight was not over. She would make one last effort to get back her husband. At least then she would have another chance to put everything right again.

*****

"Happy New Year!" Nadine grinned when Brandon opened the door of the apartment. He was already dressed in formal attire.

"Hey." Brandon hugged her to him tightly. "How are you?"

"Fine. A little jetlagged. I got in late last night." Nadine inhaled him, relaxing in the hug.

She reluctantly pulled away. In his arms felt so much like home. She had missed him like crazy for the two weeks and hadn't quite managed to forget him, despite her resolve to do so.

In fact, the opposite had happened: she thought about him every day. She was half afraid that when she got back he and his wife would be back together.

And now she felt guilty for being happy to see that he was still at the apartment and Ashley still out of the picture.

"I slept all day," she smiled at him, taking in his familiar handsome features, "but I remembered that Alisha had her thing today, so here I am."

"Yes," Brandon pulled her inside, "she is getting ready. How was the tour?"

"Great." Nadine sat down. "Tiring. I missed you." That last bit came out without warning and she didn't know where to look after such a revealing statement.

Brandon was staring at her, transfixed. "I missed you too."

"Nadine!" Ariel squealed at the doorway to the room.

Nadine was spared from a reaction to Brandon's declaration as she turned her attention to Ariel, who looked adorable in her yellow dress with little white flowers at the neckline.

"She remembers me," Nadine marveled as Ariel headed

over to her and gave her a hug.

Brandon smiled. "It seems the Blake family has a thing for you."

His statement warmed Nadine and she was still glowing long after they sat in church. Her arrival there had caused a minor stir when she followed Brandon to where his family was sitting.

His sister Latoya greeted her warmly and his mother gave her a friendly smile.

It seemed as if everything was set up for a lovely evening. It was going to be a nice way to ring in the New Year. They were going to have a candlelight service and a charge from the pastor for the New Year. She was looking forward to that. Brandon's church celebrated New Year differently from her church, and she was anticipating the experience. The music was exceptional, she was very happy to note. Because music was her business she had the tendency to be a little bit more sensitive when things were off key. This Vintage Road church had the music down pat. When Alisha sang, the entire Blake family took out their phones and cameras to record her.

And then there was a testimonies section and she stiffened in her seat when she saw Ashley walking up the aisle in a white dress. Her hair was caught up in a chignon and she looked almost ethereal and innocent.

"Brothers and sisters," Ashley said in the microphone, "I have come home. Like the old year, I have left my old life behind and I am back home where I belong, in the house of the Lord."

"No, she is not doing this," Latoya hissed. "No. Pinch me because I must be dreaming."

Nadine stiffened and so did Brandon. He was shell-shocked. His parents looked solemn too.

Ashley clutched the microphone to her, bowing her head in

a meek pose. "Like the prodigal, I have realized that things can get really rough out there and it is better to be here with fellow believers."

"Amen," the people around murmured.

"A few years ago I gave my heart to the Lord and then I strayed. That happens," Ashley bowed her head, "and I know that like the brother at home in the story of the prodigal, some of you will not like that I am back."

"The hussy is looking at me," Latoya mumbled.

"But I am back and I would like to say that my husband and I are having problems and it seems as if he has moved on, but I can't because I love him. I love my family. I love my children and I want us to be together.

"I want us to grow them up in the fear and admonition of the Lord. I know that I am partly responsible for us being apart but surely the Lord doesn't want families to break up in this manner, and so I am pleading from the bottom of my heart, Brandon, please come back home to me. I have changed. The Lord said we should forgive seventy times seven. Surely you can give me, give us another chance."

She started to cry in earnest and a big-bodied church sister went to the front and led her off the platform, hugging her as they exited through the side door.

"Fake," Latoya hissed. "I am so not impressed."

Nadine was afraid to look at Brandon, afraid to see if he was considering what Ashley said. If she was begging to be forgiven, surely he would respond.

She had all but tied his hands. She had done a confession of a sorts in the front of the church. She had even alluded to the fact that Brandon had moved on, in the process implying that it was with her, and she had begged him for forgiveness and mentioned God's forgiveness.

She could hear the whisperings about her now and

suddenly she wished that she hadn't come to witness the total breakdown of a wife who genuinely wanted her husband back and was even willing to sacrifice her pride to get him.

She was the other woman in this piece and there was no two ways about it. She stared stoically ahead but her tears were not far. She swallowed them down. Not now. Not now. She would not do this now.

*****

Brandon stepped outside of church after Ashley's stunning public confession. He did not know what to feel. Was he so jaded from years of hearing 'I am sorry and please forgive me' that he didn't feel anything?

He was hoping to find Ashley outside to find out what she was playing at, but he couldn't find her. Her car wasn't there either.

"Ashley is playing you," Latoya said, creeping up behind him.

He spun around. "I don't know. Maybe, maybe not. She made a public confession; that's not her style."

"Her style is to do whatever it takes to get you to be her slave," Latoya groaned. "Brandon, I have that girl's number. She is as fake as fake can be. She and her crocodile tears can't fool me."

Brandon sighed.

"Let her loose." Latoya urged. "Cut her loose now; don't let her hurt you again."

Brandon rubbed his hand over his eyes when he saw his mother hurrying out of the side door and looking around. He groaned, "There is the good angel."

Latoya looked around and groaned too. "I don't care if I am the bad angel. I just want you happy. You know that stress can kill. I don't want to see you stressed out and dead. Mom is squarely on Ashley's side; don't let her turn you, Brandon."

"Latoya, Ashley is my wife. I know you dislike her but the deed is done; we are married already. Maybe she and I can have a fresh start."

"You two are always having a fresh start." Latoya frowned. "Marriage is not supposed to be a battlefield, and you are always at war. Don't forget how it was. Ashley cheated on you with a girl."

Brandon winced. It took Latoya's bluntness to remind him what Ashley had done. His mother drew near and clutched his hand.

"Forgive Ashley; she made her mistakes. It's time you forgive her and start the New Year right. You have the girls. You may not know this, but living apart has affected both of them. You have always been a loving and upstanding son; you are a good Christian man, Brandon. Please find it in your heart to forgive her."

When he saw his father and Richard coming through the door, Brandon groaned. "So everyone left Nadine sitting alone?"

"She is fine. She is young and gorgeous and famous," his mother said earnestly. "She'll be fine. Maybe it was a bad idea to befriend her now. It doesn't look good either, Brandon… dating another woman when you are still married, cultivating a relationship that you know can go nowhere. The Lord gave you your own little flock to tend. You have two children, a broken home is not the legacy that you want."

His father and Richard stood nearby.

"What a way to start the New Year, huh?" Leonard chuckled dryly. "I have never in all of my life had such a dramatic start—my daughter-in-law accusing my son of moving on when she was the person at fault."

"What do you think I should do, Dad?" Brandon asked.

"Cut her loose," his father said. "I don't trust Ashley. Never did, never will. Well, unless the Lord himself impresses it upon my heart. Right now my heart is unimpressed."

"Dad is officially my favorite parent," Latoya declared, drifting closer to her father.

Beatrice sighed. "You two. I don't know what to say...we preach one thing in church and then when it comes to living, we practice something else."

Latoya made a face and then shrugged. "At the risk of sounding unchristian, I say kick the girl to the curb."

Richard moved closer to the tableau. "I think you should do a trial reconciliation. That would be a nice compromise. You have to make a serious attempt at trying to rebuild the relationship and building back the trust."

"Waste of time," Latoya murmured. "Does a leopard change its spots?"

Leonard shrugged. "That's not a bad idea, Brandon. Maybe you can see...for the kids. It never hurts to try for them, but if she goes back to treating you like a doormat, get the hell out of there—sorry for swearing," he said sheepishly, "—and don't look back."

Chapter Thirteen

For the kids...Brandon dropped a solemn-looking Nadine at his apartment; her car was there. They hadn't talked since he had left the girls at his parents' house. She was holding herself stiffly, as if she would shatter if he touched her. When he parked the car they looked over on the twinkling lights of the town that was spread before them and then Brandon turned to her. "Nadine..."

"No." Nadine shook her head. "There is no need to explain. There is no need for a speech. She is your wife. I always knew that." She looked at him and forced a smile. "I always knew that there was a possibility for reconciliation between you two."

Brandon sighed. "I have to give us one more chance."

"And that is more than okay." Nadine sighed. "That's what I like about you." Her voice cracked. She had been trying so hard to hold it together, and she didn't want to show how much his decision was hurting. "That and the fact that you are a dad who loves his children. My parents did it, you know. They stayed together for me and Tara."

"Until they couldn't do it anymore," Brandon sighed. "And then Tara became a brat."

"Maybe Tara always had that rebellious nature, who knows," Nadine mused. "Divorce affects children differently. Maybe Alisha and Ariel will be fine if you two part."

"Maybe, maybe not," Brandon mused. "I guess I owe it to them to do one more round with their mom."

"Sound happier about it," Nadine urged him, putting a note of jocularity in her voice. "I'd hate to think you are unhappy."

Brandon looked at her thoroughly, as if committing her face to memory. "You are a really lovely person. I'll never forget you."

"Thanks," Nadine croaked. She cleared her throat and got out of the vehicle quickly.

"I'll drop off the keys for the apartment tomorrow," Brandon said, a feeling of depression gripping him.

"No problem," Nadine said. "I... er... won't be there. I am spending New Year's Day with Gramps. Just leave the keys under the mat at the front."

What she really meant was that she was going to Gramps to have a good cry and she couldn't face him tomorrow.

She started the car, blinking rapidly so tears wouldn't fall. She could see Brandon leaning forlornly on the side of his car with his hands on his head. He looked so sad. Her heart broke in a million pieces.

"I love you," she whispered on a sob, driving out of the complex too fast because she didn't want him to see her tears.

*****

Brandon watched as she drove out of the complex. He could swear that he saw tears on her cheeks. It twisted something inside him. He felt bereft, as if he had lost something precious. He felt a terrible sense of loss as he watched until he couldn't see her car's taillights anymore.

Being with her these past weeks had shown him that not every male-female relationship had to be a battle. It reminded him that he could still feel again, that life didn't have to be so hard and that the best relationships were based on friendships.

Nadine had been a good friend, someone he could laugh with, confide in and just be comfortable with. They had great chemistry together. That was what he didn't have with Ashley.

He slumped on the car for ages and looked off into the darkness, but he had to let her go. He was not the type of person to maintain two relationships or to even be caught up in it.

In time he was sure that his feelings for Nadine would fade. In time, when he got caught up in his life with his family again, he would just remember her when he heard her on the radio again and maybe smile fondly.

He probably would feel a pang of jealousy whenever she got involved in a relationship or got married or had children, because he was sure that the media would carry all the highlights of her life. Gradually the jealousy would fade and life would go on. He had made a choice for his family.

He didn't trust Ashley, and he wasn't sure that he loved her anymore, nor was he sure that her confession at church was genuine, but he owed it to Alisha and Ariel to give his marriage a chance.

If he didn't have the children around, Ashley would be

history. He would be driving down after Nadine now and begging her to wait for him while he sorted out his life.

Chapter Fourteen

"**Y**ou are back!" Ashley couldn't believe that her confession at church had worked. She was genuinely surprised to see Brandon standing in the middle of the kitchen on New Year's Day with a mug in his hand, his suitcases near his feet. He was looking through the window contemplatively.

She had won. For one glowing second she considered calling Nadine Langley and gloating. *Did you think because you are a famous singer from a famous family that you could come and take my husband from me?*

She smiled wider as she thought about gloating. Nadine had looked stricken last night, with her mouth slightly opened when she had confessed. Ashley hoped that today she would be very unhappy indeed. The audacity of the girl to think that she could just move in on her family.

Brandon looked at Ashley for a long while before responding.

"Ash, it can't be like before. I am thinking of going to

Canada, and I want you and the girls to come with me. It will be a fresh start."

"Canada!" Ashley grimaced. "I don't want to move."

She watched as Brandon twisted his lips and she adjusted her stance hurriedly. She didn't want to start a fight on his first day back. She was really serious about making their relationship work.

She softened her tone. "At least not till summer. I would have a million and one things to do here before I can come. You and the girls can go without me until June."

Brandon shook his head. "Well, if you are going to be here the girls can stay in school until the summer holidays."

"OK." Ashley wasn't pleased with being saddled with the children for three whole months but she would not complain. Brandon was back. She sidled up to him and leaned on him seductively. He stiffened.

"Ash, I think we should ease back into intimacy." He stepped away from her. "I am not really over the whole Regina thing. It is something I'll be working on, okay?"

"Okay." Ashley pouted.

"And we are going back to the counselor," he warned, "or find a new one in Canada."

"Okay." Ashley nodded vigorously. "Fine, whatever you say, Brandon. I am just happy that you are home. We can go to my new counselor. She's been helping me a lot to work through my stuff."

He nodded. "Let me go unpack." He headed up the stairs. "I'll use the guest bedroom for now."

Ashley made a face. "Want us to do something for the day?"

Brandon paused on the stairs and then sighed. "I am having a slight headache; didn't sleep much last night. I think I am going to take a nap."

*****

He was not happy, Ashley mused two weeks later; it was as if he was there but not really there.

He was moping around the place as if he lost his favorite puppy. His routine in the day since he started working on private contracts was to drop the kids at school, go to whatever job he had, and then come home, looking less than happy and droopy and lost.

She had won but this didn't feel like a victory. She had him back home but this was not the Brandon that she wanted. This Brandon was downtrodden and depressed.

She looked at him now across the coffee table in the waiting room of the counselor's office, and she felt real fear. This Brandon was unreadable. He wasn't trying anymore. In the past, even at the height of all of their problems, he had been the one who was always making an effort.

She had been reassured that he would be there and that she didn't have to really pull her weight with anything, but these days she wasn't so confident that they could go back to how it was. She had this feeling of foreboding that Brandon would walk out if she put even one foot wrong. She was living on a tightrope and she wasn't used to the feeling.

She wasn't used to being so cautious around him. She wasn't used to being the pacifier. She found herself adjusting to anything he suggested, even at the expense of her precious business, because she didn't want to spook Brandon into leaving her.

She had been the one to set up the couples' counseling sessions on Tuesdays, but she had noted that he had not seemed too excited about it even though he had insisted that they needed counseling.

"Dr. Jill Hillman will see you now," the secretary said to them. Ashley got up but Brandon remained seated with his head in a magazine, looking as if he was enthralled in reading it.

"Brandon!" she hissed. "It's our turn."

"Oh." Brandon put down the magazine reluctantly and got up.

She glanced at it. It was an entertainment magazine featuring singers who sang meaningful lyrics. Nadine Langley was on the front page, along with a few other artistes.

"Lead the way." He gave her one of his functional smiles that didn't quite reach his eyes, and the thought crossed her mind that it was now, when their marriage was on the edge, that she found him even more attractive.

He was dressed in a long-sleeved green shirt with two buttons loosened at the top. The dark green color looked good on him. His neatly trimmed mustache and goatee combo made him appear even sexier than usual and his eyes—were they always such a rich chocolate brown and limpid looking, or was she just sex starved?

When they entered the office she realized that she wasn't the only one who thought that Brandon looked exceptional. The counselor actually paused when he came through the door and licked her lips slightly.

For the love of all that was holy. Ashley sat down abruptly. Her fifty-something counselor also liked her man. This was already not shaping up to be a good session.

"Ashley and Brandon." Jill shook their hands. "It's nice to meet you, Brandon," Jill smiled.

I'd say, Ashley thought snidely. *You haven't stopped staring at him since he got in here.*

"So, Brandon, I've been seeing Ashley for some time. I am happy that you can be here. Why do you think you need to be here with Ashley?"

Brandon cleared his throat and then sighed. "Ashley and I have loads of problems. The straw that broke the camel's back was when I caught her cheating on me with her friend Regina. I think we are here to repair the marriage for the children's sake."

"Ah." Jill nodded. "It's curious how you framed that. You didn't say that you want to repair the marriage because you wanted to be with Ashley."

Brandon nodded. "That's correct. I don't think I want to be with Ashley. Maybe that is another reason why I agreed to come. Maybe I can discover the spark, the trust or something for Ashley again, because God knows there is none left. I am feeling empty."

"Oh, for heaven's sake," Ashley spluttered. "He left the house after my little indiscretion and he fancies himself in love with somebody else, a home-wrecker who should know better. He was just looking at a picture of her and drooling as if he was a teenager."

The counselor looked between the two of them. "Is that true, Brandon, are you in love with somebody else?"

Brandon clasped his hands and looked down at them. He twiddled his thumbs and then shrugged. "Yes, it is."

Ashley gasped, "But why? You barely know her. How can you know somebody in six weeks?"

"I barely know you, and I lived with you for eight years," Brandon countered.

"Okay," Jill said, "calm down, you two. I can see that this will take a while for us to get through. The important thing is that you both want to save your marriage."

Brandon breathed a telling sigh and leaned back in the chair.

*****

"This is ridiculous!" Ashley had been talking since they left the counselor's office and Brandon had not heard a word. He was still marveling that he could completely tune her out. He wondered why he hadn't mastered that art years ago.

He only heard her exclaim that something was ridiculous. "What is ridiculous?" he murmured absently.

"You and your 'I'm in love with someone else crap'. You are saying it to hurt me."

Brandon turned into the driveway and spotted Regina's yellow car. He didn't feel a thing, not really. Not as devastated as he had been in the past.

He looked over at Ashley and even managed a half smile. "Your lover is here. I thought you said she was in the past… ancient history."

"She is." Ashley worried her lips between her teeth nervously. "I wonder what she is doing here. I haven't heard from her since the morning after...you know."

"Yup. I know." Brandon got out of the car and watched as Regina, who was leaning on her car and smoking a cigarette, slowly unwound herself from her relaxed pose. She turned to the two of them and sneered.

"Brandon and the lovely Ashley."

"Regina." Brandon nodded, while Ashley drifted closer to him.

Regina observed that and her expression darkened. "So, imagine my utter amazement when I found out that you two are back together."

"Are you spying on me?" Ashley asked, her voice shaky.

"I always check up on you, you know that," Regina said. "You are my girl."

Brandon watched the byplay with an utter sense of calm.

He was not the idiot he was six weeks ago who thought that he needed to fight for his relationship with Ashley at all cost. For the last couple of days he had been wondering if he wasn't wasting his time.

"I thought you were finally going to ditch this dude and the two of us could finally be together without sneaking around. So what, seeing that divorce lawyer was in vain?"

Ashley turned to Brandon. "About that—it was the day after. I honestly thought you and I were through. I was feeling guilty and.. and...and..."

Brandon nodded, feeling disinterested and curiously detached from the drama. What Regina said just now would normally have made him cringe, but now he just felt a mild revulsion.

"Leave me alone," Ashley hissed. "Just go away, Regina!"

Regina smirked. "Oh, so you think it will be that easy. I still have feelings for you and you are mine." She looked at Brandon. "I really never thought you were going to come back to her. Isn't it enough that you caught her cheating with another woman?"

"Oh, just shut up and leave," Ashley squealed. "As you can see, you are not needed here. My husband is still with me. You haven't quite managed to scare him off."

"I wonder why," Regina said slyly. "Because of the children? Which may not even be his?"

Brandon straightened up on the car. Now he was interested.

"Yes, that's right," Regina snarled. "She had an affair with a guy at the bank the same year that Alisha was born, and she had an affair when she went to Paris for her little fashion show thingy, the same year she got pregnant with Ariel. Now Brandon, even you can see that that child is not yours. Two black people can't have a mixed-race child."

"Stop this, Regina, this is ridiculous!" Ashley turned to

Brandon. "Let's ignore her. Let's just walk away from her. She's poison. She doesn't want to see me happy."

But Brandon was looking at Regina's knowing smirk, and something inside him snapped. He wanted to shut her up. He wanted her to stop hurting him with every utterance from her mouth.

He clenched his fist and advanced toward Regina, a hitherto unknown rage driving him forward.

Regina lost her casual, cocky stance and squealed fearfully, "Don't blame me for delivering the news!" She quailed at the livid fury on Brandon's face. "Ashley had an affair with Carlos King, her supervisor at the bank. She was boinking him shortly after your honeymoon, when she was supposedly a born-again Christian. And that is why I can't take her reconciliation with you seriously. Ashley is not very good with commitment, and she definitely isn't loyal."

Brandon stopped in his tracks and looked back at Ashley, who had gone still and was sobbing quietly. "I am sorry about that, Brandon. I am so sorry."

What was she saying sorry about? He needed answers and he needed them fast. He headed to Ashley and dragged her toward the house; he wasn't gentle. He didn't even care that she was in a pair of her ridiculous five-inch high heels and that she was tottering to keep up with his pace. He stopped suddenly; Ashley twisted her ankle and uttered a muffled oath.

He looked behind him at Regina, who was watching them, her mouth slightly opened.

"Get off my property," Brandon growled. "If I see you anywhere near this house again..."

Regina jumped in her car and drove out quickly. The sound of her car was the only noise besides Ashley's loud sniffling. Brandon opened the front door and pushed Ashley down into the nearest chair. She immediately kicked off her shoes.

He leaned over her. They were eyeball to eyeball; her mascara was running down her cheeks.

Brandon looked at her dispassionately. "Be honest. For once." His voice was low and rough but controlled compared to the turmoil he was feeling inside.

He now knew how it felt to want to murder someone and right here, right now, he felt as if he could happily strangle Ashley. He clenched his hand around the chair and spoke in her face. "Talk, tell me right now, all of the secrets. All of the affairs."

Ashley sniffled. "Regina was lying. She lied about everything. Can't you see that she only wants to hurt me?"

"No," Brandon gritted. "Regina may be brash and she talks tough, but with her what you see is what you get, unlike you." He shook the chair. "Tell me the truth, you lying, twisted..." He bit his tongue before he swore.

He was on the verge of losing control. He didn't even want to think about all the things that Regina said about his children not being his. He would come to that eventually. The thought lingered at the back of his mind that if that were true he would definitely kill Ashley.

He backed away from the chair and staggered into the one opposite hers. He would really do it. He could see himself doing it as soon as she opened her mouth to confirm it; he could see himself overcome with blinding rage.

He was angry enough to tear into her, right now. Two affairs—three if you counted Regina—and here he was sitting around trying to work out this marriage. He had spent eight years of his life being thoroughly fooled.

He closed his eyes and fought for control. *Lord help me!*

In the charged silence Ashley said hoarsely, "The children are yours Brandon. I wouldn't be so foolish as to give you another man's children, okay? About the affairs—I did have a thing with Carlos King at the bank but that didn't last long. It was seven years ago. I didn't want to bring it up now when we, er... are recently reconciled. I didn't have an affair with anybody in Paris. I was only there for three weeks! Where would I meet a guy and have an affair?"

Brandon squeezed his eyes shut. He couldn't believe a word that she was saying. He might never believe her again. She was a liar and she was out to ruin him. For the second time in two months, prison beckoned him.

He got up. His sister and father were right, but this time when he left he was leaving according to his own plan. He was going to see a divorce lawyer tomorrow. He believed that he had indeed reached the end of his tether. This was it—the maximum of his pain threshold.

*****

"So you left the witch for good?" Latoya asked him the next morning, He was sitting in her office after dropping the children off at school, a little later than their usual drop off time. He had stopped at A and E Genetics to get a home DNA test kit. The place wasn't open until eight and he was determined to get a sample from both Alisha and Ariel before they went to school. He had swabbed them right there in the parking lot of the genetics lab and returned the kit to them for assessment before taking the children to school.

It was going to take him two to three days to get the results. He felt restless. He had to know if they were his. He had looked at each of them this morning for the longest time, and the necessity of a DNA test had only made him feel angrier toward Ashley.

He zoned into what Latoya was saying and nodded. "Yes,

I am ready for Kenneth's number. I understand that this can take me up to a year. I want to just get it over with."

"What did she do to tick you off this time?" Latoya pulled her chair closer to the desk and leaned on her arm, looking at him.

Brandon didn't answer. He clenched his jaw and forcibly told himself to relax. Every time he thought about the possibility of Ashley hoodwinking him through the years he felt angrier and angrier. Last night he hadn't slept a wink. He had sat outside on the balcony of the guest room and just stared into space until daybreak. He had never felt this unsettled in his life.

"Some women are not marriage material," he said contemplatively. "I can't fathom why Ashley wanted to marry me in the first place. Why me?"

He sighed and looked at his sister. "I am a good man, or at least I try to be. I am always trying to do things God's way, and I get blindsided by this."

"Ah Brandon," Latoya sighed, "she fooled us all. She is a really good actress."

"But couldn't God have stopped me?" Brandon asked, "I mean couldn't he have warned me?"

Then he remembered that God had warned him in so many ways. Last night he had thought about them. There was the time when she had walked into church, beautiful, extremely attractive, and he had found himself slightly repulsed. That was not a normal reaction for a man to have.

And when she had started coming to Bible Studies he had the feeling that she was not genuine. That had been quickly suppressed when she had seemed to know the scriptures pretty well.

The pastor counseling them had told him not to do it. His own father had looked him squarely in the face on his wedding day and told him that if he changed his mind, there was no shame in not going through with the wedding.

He hadn't listened. He had gotten gentle promptings and outright shoves and he hadn't listened.

He got up. "Latoya, I have a ton of things to do but the chief thing today is to see Kenneth."

"Yes, Here is the number." Latoya wrote it down hurriedly. "Call me. Don't you dare internalize this and suffer alone."

*****

Kenneth's office was on the same office block as Alisha and Ariel's dentist. Brandon had called ahead and when he reached the office the receptionist gave him a pleasant smile and told him, "Mr. Welch will see you now."

Brandon entered the spacious office and sat down. Kenneth was a jovial guy with a pleasant smile.

After the pleasantries he said to Brandon, "Here's the thing: divorce in Jamaica is not easy or quick. It takes exceptional circumstances for a person to get a quickie divorce, or if you personally know a judge who will not take forever to sign the decree nisi. The decree absolute takes only a few weeks after that.

"Luckily for you, I know quite a few judges I can lean on to expedite things a bit. I am known as the man to get you the quickest divorce done. This could take six to eight months instead of the usual year if you retain me as your legal counsel. I assume there is property involved, and children?"

"Yes," Brandon said, feeling slightly overwhelmed.

It just dawned on him that he was sitting in a lawyer's office discussing divorce. The cessation of his marriage to Ashley. He should feel odd about it, but he had this burning desire to just get it over and done with.

"Is there any hope of reconciliation?" Kenneth asked.

"Oh no." Brandon shook his head. "Never. We already tried that several times."

Kenneth cleared his throat. "Good. So we are going to have to talk division of assets and custodial rights to your children."

Brandon nodded.

"But we don't have to do that now," Kenneth said quickly, "this is the part where negotiations may stretch out for a while."

"Well," Brandon said, "she can keep her store; that's all she cares about anyway. I want the house and kids or alternatively to sell the house and give her half of the proceeds. I don't think I want to ever live there again."

"Unusual," Kenneth said contemplatively.

"I am planning on leaving Jamaica for a while, so those are my demands. I really don't want to have anything to do with Ashley after this."

"Except that you have children," Kenneth said. "Unfortunately for you, man, that is a bond for life. She'll always be the mother of your children."

Chapter Fifteen

Ashley came home earlier than usual. She had had a raging headache for four straight days since Regina had come back into her life and derailed it, again. Brandon was treating her like a pariah.

He didn't even pretend as if he wanted to talk to her anymore. He was giving her the silent treatment. He wouldn't even make an effort with her in front of the kids, which was making her fret because each morning she got up early enough to join them at breakfast, hoping that at least with the children there he would talk to her and try to appear normal. He didn't seem much impressed by that.

The first morning she had attempted to talk, Brandon had told her that he didn't speak hypocrite.

She popped two migraine pills in her mouth and swallowed them with her bottled water and closed her eyes. She needed to plan a new strategy to win back Brandon. She needed to do something before she really lost him for good. Their last bust-up had not been encouraging in that regard.

The ringing of the bell from the postman had her cracking her eyes open. She watched as he put a bundle of mail in the mailbox at the gate and then drove away. She couldn't recall being home this early to actually see the postman delivering mail.

Through the years she had quarreled whenever Brandon left a monetary gift for him at Christmas. She thought it was excess; after all, he was just doing his job.

She got out of the car and headed to the letterbox, pulling out the fistful of letters, and walked slowly to the house.

How had her life come to this?

Really. How?

She once had it all: an attentive husband who loved her to distraction and would do anything for her...now she was the one who was fighting to keep their marriage together.

She threw the bundle of letters on the side table for Brandon to deal with as usual but then the words A and E Genetics caught her eye.

Genetics Laboratory.

She picked it up and leaned on the wall. No, he didn't. She felt a cold hand of fear clasp her heart; she was so weak with it that she slumped on the wall. Why was Brandon doing this to her? It was unconscionable. He had changed so much. At least he used to take her word for things. Now he was actually checking up on what she said, like he was some sort of super sleuth.

She opened the letter with shaking hands and then read through it.

She heard footsteps at the top of the stairs and she shoved it in her bag. She hadn't realized that Brandon was even around. By the time he had appeared at the top of the stairs and was making his way down, she had kicked off her shoes and arranged herself on the settee with her hand on top of her head.

Brandon didn't even say hi to her as he sifted through the letters. She watched him as he looked through each one with a disappointed frown on his face.

Well, good for you, Ashley thought waspishly. *How dare you question my integrity?*

She felt Brandon's eyes on her as he spun around.

"Ashley." His voice was harsh, as usual. Was he any way else these days?

"Yes," she whispered. "My head is pounding; can you keep your voice down a notch?"

"No," Brandon shouted. "Where is the letter from A and E Genetics?"

Ashley opened her eyes wide. "What letter?"

Brandon sighed. "You never bring in the mail. Never. You usually leave it up to me. Now, where is that letter? They said it would be here today."

Ashley groaned. "Seriously, Brandon, it is the first day that I have ever seen the postman. I have a headache but I decided to get the post and save you the trip. I am changing a bit, aren't I? I am trying to save our marriage and proving to you that I can change. This is just one of the things that constitutes the new Ashley. I get home early and I get the post. I put them there, on the side table where you always put them. What is A and E Genetics--is that an engineering firm?"

Brandon sighed. "I don't know how I spent so long listening to that exact same voice speaking in such innocence and not suspecting a thing."

He advanced toward her bag and Ashley shot up off the settee and pulled it to her.

Brandon growled. "Just give me the letter!"

"No!" Ashley shouted. "I can't believe that you went behind my back and tested the children, disbelieving what I told you four days ago. That is so low, Brandon." She pulled the letter out of the bag and started tearing it up. "I am not that person, the one that you are implying that I am. I may be everything else that you are calling me, a cheater, a liar—whatever—but to imply that I could give you not one but two children from two other men...it's ridiculous. So your little DNA test was just the lowest thing you have ever done to me."

Brandon watched in shock as she meticulously tore up the page into pieces, squashed it into a ball, and threw it at him.

"Are you happy that you humiliated me now?" Ashley screamed. "You are constantly dragging me through the mud. So I had an affair donkey ages ago. It fizzled out. Men do it to women all the time; you guys are notorious for it. I did it and I am sorry. It won't happen again, but to actually imply that my children are not yours is really low. Really low!"

She got up and headed for the stairs. She looked back at him balefully. "I never expected this from you, Brandon."

Brandon looked at the bundle of paper at his feet and slowly stooped to pick it up.

*****

He pushed it in his pocket and went to his office. He passed the room door. He could hear Ashley in the room crying, big heaving sobs that were loud enough to wake the dead.

He wasn't impressed by it or her little speech earlier. He knew her penchant for melodrama quite well and he wasn't overly impressed with her little show just now. He sat around the desk and laid out the crushed bundle of paper on his desk. One by one he smoothed the pieces out. He would painstakingly put them back together if it took him all day.

He had to see for himself if those children were really his and if he couldn't piece back the paper together, there was always the electronic version, and if they didn't send that, he was going to do another test. He couldn't trust Ashley again and even though she had looked genuinely distressed when she found out about the test, he was not going to let that fool him.

But the papers proved to be thoroughly shredded. It was like piecing together a jigsaw puzzle; Ashley had really done a good job of tearing up the paper, as if she was truly gripped with righteous indignation. The paper seemed as if it had a chart on it. He was not going to be able to read it. The scientific terms eluded him; he wouldn't know what to look for.

He opened his laptop. He had asked them to both post the letter and send him the results via email. He opened his mail. His hands trembled involuntarily when he saw that there was a mail from them.

He clicked on the mail. There was the chart again, STR Locus, Allele Range… He scanned that impatiently and headed to the Statement of Results.

"Finally."

"Based on the DNA analysis Brandon Blake is excluded as the biological father of Alisha Blake because they do not share sufficient genetic markers. The probability of the relationship is indicated below…"

He looked below. "Probability 0%."

He went through and read the other part numbly. "Based on the DNA analysis Brandon Blake is excluded as the biological father of Ariel Blake...probability 0%."

He leaned back in his chair.

Zero percent to both. Regina had been right, and now his worst nightmare was fulfilled.

A pain clutched his chest from nowhere and he gasped with the intensity of the feeling. He took deep gulps of air and tried to ease the pain. This was not really happening. He had really been a doormat, a whipped, total idiot for the past couple of years being married to Ashley.

Ashley...he couldn't think about Ashley right now. His first instinct was to bang on the door, haul her out by her hair and demand to know the truth. Who was Alisha's father? Was it that guy she had that affair with, and who was Ariel's father?

Who the hell were they? How on earth could she have unprotected sex with various men while they were married and have the audacity to believe that he wouldn't ever find out about the biggest lie of all?

He clenched and unclenched his fist. His heart was racing alarmingly. He could have a heart attack right here, right now in his office, if he didn't calm down.

And then he thought of the girls. The girls he was raising as his own. The girls he thought were his. He had never been biologically related to them.

"Oh Lord." He put his head in his hands and felt the tears prickling his eyes. Those girls meant the world to him.

He had spent a few more years than he should have in an unhealthy marriage because of them, and they weren't even his.

He had been tied to Ashley because of them. He had tried to save his marriage because of them. He had lived a sub-par existence, being chronically unhappy, because of them. He had been both their mom and dad, staying up nights when they were teething and needed soothing. Kissing childhood booboos and playing with them, making sure that they were happy and healthy. Protecting them, providing for them and they weren't even his.

He gulped down a sob.

What would he do now about them?

He already knew that the marriage was over, but what about them? Could he just leave them in Ashley's care like that? How on earth would they grow up? Try as he might, he couldn't think of them as other than his right now.

Maybe that would change in the future but for right now... he closed the computer screen and got up.

He had to get out of this house this evening. He would drive to Negril to Richard's place for a few days. He had to give this house a break. He had to think without kids... without wife...he had to go for his sanity's sake.

*****

Brandon packed light and drove to the West coast. He deliberately kept the radio on the BBC and actually took comfort in hearing about the problems from the different areas in the world to take his mind off his. When they brought on a feature about a new engineering technique he listened keenly, grateful for the respite from his thoughts.

When he got near Richard's cottage, he called his sister. Though they referred to the place as a cottage, and it was finished in a rustic charm that could easily fool you into thinking that you were living the simple life, it was part of a community of nine other luxurious cottages with a private beach in the back yard. The security guard at the gate and the caretaker could only let him in with Richard or Latoya's permission.

His sister picked up the phone on the first ring.

"Brandon! What's going on? The witch called Mom and she claims that she is sick and apparently claimed that you made her so. She also claimed that you stormed out of the house because of some petty quarrel and that there was nobody there to pick up the kids from school."

Brandon pulled over on the side of the road. His blood began to boil again when he heard Ashley's name.

"I am in Negril. I am going to chill out at the cottage for the rest of the week. Can you tell the caretaker?"

"Sure." Latoya had a frown in her voice. "But what happened today? What did she do now?"

Brandon bit his lip from responding. "I don't...I really don't want to talk about it."

"Okay, fine." Latoya sounded offended. "You can talk to me, you know."

Brandon sighed. "Lats, if I talk right now, I crack. I have been holding it together all evening driving down. Just call the caretaker, please."

"Okay," Latoya said sympathetically. "Mom went to pick up Alisha and Ariel."

"Good," Brandon said. "That's good."

"And they are staying with her tonight," Latoya added. "I know they mean the world to you, so I have to report. What should we tell them about you not being around?"

"Tell them I took a vacation," Brandon said, fresh pain lancing him at the thought that just a few hours ago he thought they were his children biologically and now they weren't.

"You must be really out of it," Latoya said, "that you forgot the girls when you stormed out today. Give me a call and check in at least a day or two so I don't worry, all right?"

"Fine." Brandon hung up the phone from Latoya and pulled back out onto the road. No, he hadn't forgotten the girls; he had been thinking about them when he did.

*****

The cottage was just the antidote that his pained senses needed. He received the keys from the caretaker, Mr. Binns, who informed him that the place was so clean he could eat from the floor.

He let himself into the cottage and breathed a sigh of relief. He could hear the sea outside as it lashed the shore. It was just two hundred feet away. He could also hear the crickets.

They seemed louder in Negril than in Kingston. He looked around the designer rustic cottage, with its bright, airy wood-finished interior. Some of the posts even had carvings in them. He walked around one which had faces and leaves and vines wrapped around it. He had been to the cottage several times, but the carved wooden posts were always a pleasure to look at.

He went to the small kitchenette and looked in the cupboards. Latoya always kept it stacked with non-perishables. Tomorrow he would plug in the fridge. Or maybe not. He could always eat at the restaurant on the compound. They did meals to order.

He picked up the menu, thinking he should order something, but then he changed his mind. Tomorrow he would have a big breakfast. He lay on the bed. He wished there was some magical way to switch off his mind and not think. He had thought that the most devastating thing that could happen to a man was finding out that his wife was cheating on him with a woman, but he now realized that that did not compare to what Ashley had done through the years.

She made him love them and take care of them. Couldn't she have just had some pity on him and left him when she had the first affair? He would have been hurt then, but it would have saved him years of heartache.

He fell asleep sometime after that and was awakened by music. He glanced at the clock and groaned. It was six-thirty in the morning and the music sounded as if it were coming from a live band.

He recognized the song, "Break My Stride." His sister used to joke that she told Richard the lines of the chorus when they were just dating back in university. *Ain't nobody gonna break my stride, ain't nobody gonna hold me down, I gotta keep on moving...*

He got up when he recognized that the voice singing was most definitely Nadine Langley's.

His heart swelled with longing. He missed her. He hadn't stopped. She was not just someone he had liked just because he was hurting.

He had loved everything about her. Nadine was a famous singer, yet she was refreshingly normal and grounded.

When he heard somebody yell 'cut' and the music stop, he got up and looked out. There were quite a few people down by the beach. They had equipment spread around. The sun hadn't even come out properly yet. He went out on the porch and Mr. Binns quickly came by, giving him a hurried good morning.

"What's happening?" Brandon asked him.

"Gramps Langley and Nadine Langley are doing two music videos here on our compound. They've been here since yesterday; they are just finishing up. Don't worry, the noise will be down by ten. I should have told you last night; sorry for the inconvenience."

Brandon nodded. The air was chilly. He could see Nadine now; she had people surrounding her before but now he could clearly make her out on the sea side. She was in a floaty white dress, and somebody was applying makeup to her face. They arranged her hair. The director called action and the music started again.

He contemplated going out to reintroduce himself to her. Maybe she had forgotten him. He wasn't that memorable, just a guy who she had taken pity on and hung out with when he was hurting about his sham of a marriage. She must have moved on by now and written him off as a complete waste of six weeks of her life.

He went back into the cottage and showered. He was going to head to the restaurant and order a big breakfast and lie in the hammock that was tied between two sea-grape trees that were at the side of the cottage and try to get lost in one of the many novels that his sister had in the bookcase.

He stepped onto the stone pathway and had all intentions of heading to the main cabin when he looked over by the beach side. They seemed as if they were finished, the lighting people were taking down their equipment and the band was standing around and laughing.

He debated with himself whether he should go over and say something when he saw a guy dressed in full black who looked like one of the crew go over to Nadine and say something in her ear, and she started giggling. The guy had his arm around her familiarly, like he had a right to do so.

Brandon turned toward the cabin. That was it; she didn't need him in her life with his million and one woes. She was happy, young and carefree. Obviously she had forgotten him already, as it should be.

When he was her age, he had thought that he was happy and young and carefree too; with a wife by his side, both of them would conquer the world. They would be the best family ever, an example to the neighborhood, a pillar of the church, but that was the year when his wife had most certainly been having an affair with a guy at her bank and had gotten pregnant by him.

My God, would he ever... ever forget that?

The thought that he didn't have any biological children hit him when he sat down at a table in the back of the restaurant where he could look out at the sea.

He didn't even know if he was capable of having any. His parents didn't have any biological grandchildren either. Alisha and Ariel weren't blood relatives. They were not really Blakes.

"We have a special this morning," a young waiter smiled at him, a note pad in hand, "or do you want a more continental breakfast?"

"What's on the special?" Brandon asked. He didn't know if he could even eat. His appetite had fled.

"Fried dumplings, ackee and salt fish and avocado," the guy said, "and we have a selection of various beverages, juices, tea..."

Brandon nodded. "Orange juice with the special. Thanks."

"Okey doke," the waiter said, jotting down on his notepad, and then he looked up. "The crew is coming. Yesterday they had breakfast with us—Nadine Langley and Gramps Langley."

He went away swiftly and Brandon looked back out at the sea. He was happy that his back was turned to the doorway. Maybe Nadine would not even acknowledge him anyway.

He didn't glance their way when the crew filled up the tiny restaurant; he heard the buzz of conversation around him and the healthy laughter. The waiter brought his food and drinks and hurried away. It was buzzing in the open space.

The scent of the food brought his appetite back and he dug in.

"Is this seat taken?" He looked up and saw that it was her. She was still in that white dress and her face was bare of makeup, like she had scrubbed it off. She looked so dear to him that his chest constricted.

"No," he swallowed his food.

Nadine smiled at him. "Good."

She sat down and he watched her every move with fascination.

"How are you?" she asked, giving him one of her melting smiles.

"Terrible," he wanted to say but with her sitting across from him, he couldn't say that. He was feeling remarkably light and pleased to see her, like she was the light at the end of the dark and dank tunnel that was his life.

"I am good, now." He added the now deliberately. "Seeing you, I mean."

"And how are your wife and the girls?"

Brandon sighed and put down his fork.

"Uh-oh," Nadine raised a brow. "Trouble in paradise again?"

"Something like that," Brandon said. "It was never paradise, you know."

Nadine nodded. "Obviously. It's what, three weeks since you two got back together, and now you are apart again?"

"Yup," Brandon said, "and this time I filed for divorce."

"You did?" Nadine looked at him solemnly. "Want to talk about it? I was your friend, remember?"

"We were a little more than that," Brandon said softly. "We had feelings for each other."

"No," Nadine shook her head. "I had feelings for you. You were on the rebound."

"No, I wasn't." Brandon stared in her sparkling eyes, and a feeling of rightness washed over him.

Whenever he saw her or talked to her, he couldn't help but feel that they would be right together. It made him wish that he had waited for her, instead of getting married to Ashley.

But maybe he wouldn't have met her. Maybe life was exactly as it should be.

"So have you moved on?" Brandon asked. "This morning I saw you; you looked happy and carefree and there was that guy whispering in your ear."

Nadine laughed. "That was Karl."

She pointed to him, sitting at the table with other crew members. They had on black shirts with white lettering 'crew' across the front.

"Karl Langley, my cousin. He produces videos for us."

Karl waved to them and Brandon waved back.

"I like it that you were jealous," Nadine said, smiling. "I spent the better part of the last three weeks telling myself that it is completely uncool to be grieving over a married man."

"I thought you had forgotten me by now." Brandon touched her hand and then laced his fingers with hers.

"Maybe I will in a year or so or maybe two years," Nadine said wearily. "I was giving myself two years."

Brandon laughed. "I missed you. I thought about you every day. Something would remind me of your laughter or that way you tilt your head when you are considering something."

"I missed you too," Nadine said. "Remember when we used to just talk and talk about everything and nothing? I got used to that."

"Maybe we can do that again?" Brandon asked.

"No," Nadine said regretfully. "The problem with loving a married man is that there is always the possibility of him getting back with his wife. You two have kids together; I can't be the one who comes between you and your family, Brandon. I can't do it. It would kill me."

"Yeah," Brandon cleared his throat, "about that...we need

to talk. I am not going to change my mind about divorcing Ashley, that's for sure."

Nadine smiled and squeezed his fingers. She looked down at their clasped hands earnestly. "Well, until the ink is dry on your divorce papers. I am not going to take anything for granted."

"Fair enough." Brandon raised her hand and kissed it.

Chapter Sixteen

The kiss made it to the *Real News*, a weekend gossip rag that was widely read because of its sometimes inaccurate gossip and innuendos. The waiter had snapped a picture of Nadine and Brandon and sold it to the paper and somebody had done a little private investigation.

And that was the picture that greeted Ashley at her desk on Friday morning. She read *Real News* avidly because of the juicy little tidbits she got from that and the gossipy news about celebrity lives; besides, she advertised with them. She didn't expect that Brandon would be on the front page kissing Nadine Langley's hand.

She sat down at her desk hard. She hadn't seen him since Tuesday. He hadn't even called home. She had left the children with his parents for the week, feigning sickness, because she honestly didn't want to have to deal with them and their questions about Daddy and when he was coming home.

Such a huff about her tearing up his crazy little DNA testing paper. He didn't even know what the DNA results were and he had stormed off again. She didn't know what the results were either and to be honest, it had given her a few sleepless nights. She didn't have enough time to read the results.

At least Alisha must be his. Carlos had gotten a vasectomy years before their affair. Ariel she wasn't so sure about. She had had a stupid drunken one-night stand with a male model in Paris. She didn't even remember the guys name; he was Pietre, or Petre or something like that. The sex had not even been good. It had been over in no time. He had left her hotel room after and she hadn't seen him since. She doubted she would even remember who he was.

She looked down at the paper. That was not an affair. That had been a huge mistake that she did not even want to think about.

She stared at the picture of Brandon and Nadine. Why whenever he was with her did he look so darn happy and relaxed. He was staring at her as if she was the only woman in the world.

He seemed to love her, and that was sickening to her.

She recognized the wood railing and the sea in the background; they had been at the restaurant on the property in Negril where Richard owned one of those luxurious cottages. It was a nice place to go to unwind.

Ashley gritted her teeth and read the headline: *Local Celebrity Sheds her Squeaky Clean Image with a Bang*. In lower case letters it read *Nadine Langley has an affair with a married man.*

Ashley groaned. How could Brandon do this to her? He was crazy if he thought he was going to humiliate her in public with Nadine Langley.

That was what he was doing, humiliating her with this. He

had no moral authority now to talk to her about affairs.

So there. Now they were even. Maybe now they could move on with their lives.

Jaya came to the door. "Is it true, is Brandon having an affair with Nadine Langley? Is that why you two are breaking up? I can't believe I work for you and I have to find out the juicy tidbits of your life from a newspaper.

"The article says that Nadine caused a breakup between you two and that Brandon was living in her apartment in Smoky Vale for a while and that his church pastor spoke to him and that he moved back home but he is still continuing his affair."

"That's what it said?" Ashley asked incredulously.

"Yes," Jaya came farther into the room. "There is also a piece about you being a longsuffering wife and that Brandon has cheated on you in the past. It even said that he has filed for divorce."

"For the love of..." Ashley halted mid-exclamation. It suddenly dawned on her that the paper was making out Brandon to be the bad guy and she was the innocent wife who was being cheated on. She would have to peruse the article later and check to see if they mentioned the store. Now that would be a nice bonus.

She adjusted her expression and smiled at Jaya sadly. "I didn't want my life to be splashed all over the papers. This is between Brandon and me."

"And Nadine," Jaya pointed out.

"And her." Ashley spat. "Do we have a number for her studio on file? Maybe I should call that home-wrecker and put her in her place."

"You should," Jaya encouraged. "Or better yet, confront her. I don't care who it is, the other woman should not believe that she can just come and break up your happy home just like that. Just because she's a big singer, she thinks she can come and mess with you."

"Yes," Ashley said, "you know what? You call her studio and find out if she is there. I can go there and give her a visit. I'll do so this morning."

"You go, girl," Jaya said, getting up.

*****

Nadine was sitting in Tenaj's office while she shouted to whoever was on the phone line.

"This is libelous. Nadine Langley is not having an affair. If you do not retract this stupid headline, I am going to make sure that you never print another word again. You hear me?"

She slammed down the phone and looked over at Nadine, who was grinning.

"What on earth are you laughing about?" Tenaj asked, exasperated. "Nearly a hundred thousand persons are reading this piece of trash and are thinking that you are a home-wrecker. You are now the source of gossip for hundreds of lunchrooms across Jamaica."

"Which is not necessarily bad marketing. It's kind of funny, though," Nadine said. "At the time that picture was taken we were discussing how I am not going to be a home-wrecker. We ate breakfast together. We said our goodbyes. I left with the crew and Brandon said he'd stay in touch. He was going to spend the rest of the day vegetating in a hammock."

"Well," Tenaj shrugged. "it's not necessarily bad marketing, but your reputation… I hate for this kind of thing to be associated with the Langley brand."

"He's getting a divorce," Nadine said.

"I'll believe it when I see it," Tenaj scoffed. "Married men always say that. What did Ashley do to make him run away like a chicken this time, buy the wrong brand of cereal?"

"He didn't say," Nadine said, exasperated. "I don't think Ashley is the good guy in all of this, Tenaj. If you saw him, he looked so sad..."

Before Tenaj could respond her phone rang. She held up her finger. "Hold that thought," and picked it up.

When she put it back down, she had a look of shock on her face. "Well, speaking of the devil or angel, whichever way you want to look at it, Ashley is in the lobby area waiting to see you."

"Me!" Nadine squeaked. "Why?"

Tenaj raised her brow. "Because of the stupid article in *Real News*."

Nadine grimaced. "I hope she is not out there to give me a beat down, because I can't fight and I am not having an affair with her husband."

When Nadine walked to the lounge area, Ashley was sitting there looking pretty and dressed in a pink power suit and nude heels.

She got up when she saw Nadine and towered over her in her heels. "Is there somewhere we can talk?"

No greeting. Nadine nodded. "Sure. The boardroom is through here."

Ashley followed her to the boardroom, her heels making dainty clicking sounds on the floor tiles.

When they were in the boardroom she turned to Nadine. "Let's cut to the chase, Nadine. I don't know what Brandon has told you about me."

"Nothing much," Nadine said. "We never really talk about you."

"Is that so?" Ashley sniffed. "I guess when a man is having an affair, the topic of his wife would be a conversation killer."

"We are not having an affair." Nadine shrugged. "The

paper is rubbish."

Ashley snorted. "I never believed it, really. Brandon told me that he loved you some weeks ago, though, and that is concerning for me."

Nadine gasped. "He did? He said that!"

"Yes." Ashley sat down in one of the chairs. "I wish to God he'd just have an affair with you and forget you but no, he has feelings for you. That, to me, is unacceptable. It hurts. And he knows it would hurt."

Nadine sat down on a chair across from Ashley as well. Brandon loved her. She loved him too. The situation would be perfect if not for this woman sitting before her.

"I am going to ask you woman to woman," Ashley said earnestly, "just leave my husband alone, please." Her eyes filled with water and Nadine remembered how she had pleaded with Brandon to come back home on New Year's Eve.

"I have not troubled him," Nadine said softly. She was feeling a little guilty, though, because through the weeks when she had no contact with Brandon she had missed him fiercely, like a limb was missing. "We were doing a video shoot by Sea Wind Cottages and he was staying there. We had breakfast that morning. I haven't heard from him since."

"Oh," Ashley said.

"We, the whole crew, left at the same time."

"Oh," Ashley said again.

"Listen," Nadine said, "obviously you guys have problems. Brandon has never shared your problems with me."

Ashley nodded. "I see. Yes, we do have some issues but it is nothing that can't be sorted out with time and attention. For Brandon to go and form new attachments outside of our marriage is so unlike him. I love him, you know. I always have, from the moment I saw him, and I think I always will.

I want him back. I want my family back to where it used to be."

It was Nadine's turn to nod. She felt like Ashley had thrown a heavy burden on her, like she was somehow responsible for her and Brandon breaking up. She knew that couldn't be true. When she had first met Brandon he had left their house.

"Well then," Ashley said, "thank you for the talk."

"You are welcome." Nadine walked with her outside. When Ashley drove away, she felt a sense of dread.

"I didn't hear any scuffling," Tenaj said, "and I had my ears to the door."

Nadine sighed. "Ashley said that Brandon told her that he loves me."

"He did. What an inconsiderate husband," Tenaj huffed.

"I think I am the reason that they broke up the second time around," Nadine said tiredly. "I don't want that, Tenaj. I can't live with being the reason that a man would leave his family but the truth is I am kind of happy too, because I love him, but now I can't be with him."

She inhaled roughly. "I can't be the reason. If we end up together I would forever be wondering what if he does it to me as well."

"Oh come here." Tenaj hugged her.

Her phone rang at the same time and she looked at the call display. It was an unknown number.

She answered cautiously, "Hello."

"Hi Nadine. This is Latoya, Brandon's sister."

"Hi Latoya." Nadine tensed up for a cussing.

Latoya laughed. "You say that so cautiously. Anyway, on Saturday night we are having a little send off party for Brandon. He leaves next week Wednesday for Canada, as you may know."

"No, I didn't." Her voice cracked. He was leaving. The

thought gave her a pang of regret.

"The party will be at our parents' place. If you give me your email address I'll send the invite."

Nadine cleared her throat. "Latoya, I can't. I don't want to intrude on Brandon's life any more than I have to."

"It is no intrusion at all," Latoya said. "Alisha and Ariel are looking forward to seeing you. They insisted that you come."

"Oh." Nadine closed her eyes. What harm would it do if she went to a party to tell Brandon goodbye, for good? "Okay, then I'll be there."

"Good," Latoya said.

"I am not having an affair with your brother," Nadine said hurriedly.

"Oh, I know that," Latoya laughed. "I know my brother. Whoever wrote the article was painting Ashley as a saint. I found it more comical than serious. See you Saturday night."

Chapter Seventeen

Brandon reluctantly left Negril on Saturday evening. He knew he had to get back to Kingston and face the music, pack for Canada and do some last minute arrangements, but he was not looking forward to going back home.

Home. Where was that, really?

He had only had a couple days to get used to the idea that his life as he knew it was a sham. His wife was rotten to the core; his children weren't his. Every time he thought that, fresh pain lanced him. And he had thought about nothing but that for the five days he had spent in Negril. He couldn't even bring himself to call the children.

He could imagine Alisha's stern face as she took him to task about not calling him for five whole days. He inhaled and then exhaled. He was no closer to a solution to his dilemma than he was when he went to Negril.

He envisioned two scenarios: he gave up all rights to them and walked out of their lives without an explanation, cut off all links. He could quit them cold turkey. He would let Ashley figure out what to tell them, but somehow that didn't sit well with him.

He could not do that to them. They depended upon him for a stable family life. He was really all they had. If he left they would be devastated.

Or he could have them full time with him, without Ashley involved in their lives. That would not be anything new for them, unfortunately. He wanted to divorce Ashley and completely sever all ties with her.

He wanted full custody of the girls. Maybe someday when he had calmed down and mellowed out sufficiently he could think of them visiting her but for now...no way.

He would have to adopt them to have some legal foot to stand on, especially if he were going to migrate, because they were not his biologically.

He couldn't for the life of him see any middle ground right now. He wasn't going to share custody or give Ashley maintenance money to spend on them.

This divorce had to be done his way. If Ashley thought that she even had a foot to stand on or even made a murmur about anything, he would out her for the nasty piece of work she was.

His anger fueled him all the way to Kingston. He stopped at his mother's house as his sister had requested and was surprised to see so many cars there.

The place was dark, though. He walked up the steps, frowning. The door was opened when he stepped on the porch, the lights came on, and a sea of faces met him with a shout. "Surprise!"

Brandon jumped. He was genuinely surprised.

"Hey, little brother," Latoya came out of the crowd. "It's your surprise going away party."

"I can't believe it." Brandon tried hard to put a smile on his face; he was not in the mood to party.

When Alisha and Ariel made a beeline for him, he bent and picked them up. Weak, treacherous tears came to his eyes. When he hugged them he buried his face in Alisha's neck. They were his. He inhaled their scent, kissing them loudly on their cheeks.

Scenario number one was out the window. He didn't know if he could love them any more, and he couldn't walk away from them. Not now. Maybe not ever.

"Daddy!" Alisha looked at him her eyes wide. "You didn't call all week."

"Come now, honey," his mother took Ariel, who was clinging to him like a limpet. "You will have your daddy for a couple more days."

"It won't happen again." Brandon looked at Alisha solemnly.

She looked at him for the longest while and then nodded, reassured.

His mother carried the children away. "It's near their bedtime, but they had to see you."

"I'll come and tuck them in," Brandon said.

He was pulled around to the back of the house, which was set up for a party, twinkling lights with tables and chairs scattered throughout the lawn.

He spotted people from church, his friends from school and Nadine.

He blinked and saw that it really was her. She was in a yellow dress which fit her slim frame like a second skin. Before he could head in her direction he was stopped several times by several of his friends and acquaintances.

Richard stopped him before he could drift nearer to her. "Did you see the headlines on *Real News*?"

"No," Brandon frowned. "Didn't read a paper or watch the news these past couple of days."

"Well, they saw you guys in Negril. You were kissing her hand and they implied that the two of you were having an affair. Well, not implied—they said it out right."

Brandon groaned. "Really?"

"Yup," Richard said, "so if you see some of your church friends looking at you funny, that's why."

Brandon chuckled. "How ironic."

"I know." Richard slapped him on the back. "I think you need this time away in Canada to get yourself sorted."

"I do," Brandon sighed.

"Latoya was cut up that you wouldn't say why you left Ashley this time around," Richard continued.

"Your wife needs to be less nosy." Brandon rejoined.

Richard laughed.

He finally made his way over to Nadine, who was surrounded by an adoring group.

"Hi," he said.

"Hey," she smiled but the smile didn't quite reach her eyes.

"What's wrong?" Brandon asked.

"I'll tell you later." She inclined her head. "You look good. The couple of days in Negril was needed, wasn't it? You lost that haggard edge."

"Yes, it was needed."

The noise and talking and laughter around them ebbed, and Brandon spun around. The place was almost deathly quiet. He saw why when Ashley made her way through the throng, dressed in a virginal white sleeveless dress. She headed for him, a slant on her lips.

She was planning to make a spectacle of them. Brandon could feel it, because he knew that Latoya would not invite her to a party that she had planned.

He didn't have long to wait before the hysterics began.

"Brandon, I can't believe that you are having a party and I was not invited but your mistress was."

Brandon looked at Nadine, who looked as if she shrank a little bit inside. She was embarrassed.

Ashley was playing to the gallery. And he was tired of it. He was tired of being the fall guy; he was tired of protecting Ashley and her reputation when she had no qualms with trampling over his.

"Ashley," he gritted, "leave before I say something to this crowd that you'll regret."

"What can you say?" Ashley's lips trembled. "I have not done anything wrong. I am the wife who loves you, while you carry out your little affair with Nadine behind my back."

Brandon looked around. His mother and father were standing close by. His mother had her hand over her mouth in shock; his father looked indifferent. Richard was holding back Latoya, and he almost grinned at the fierceness in his sister's eyes. Nadine had slithered away into the group to his right. She looked stricken.

"Okay," he said out loud, "you asked for this showdown in a public place. Well people, here is the truth. Ashley and I broke up first because I found her in bed with her friend Regina. They were not resting. I am sure I don't need to spell out what they were doing in our marital bed. Did I say that it was in our marital bed?"

There were gasps all around.

Ashley recoiled. "What the hell are you doing?"

"You asked for it," Brandon said.

"He's lying," Ashley snarled. "Brandon, why are you doing this to me? I am the mother of your children."

And then something snapped in him. There it was again, that term 'mother of his children'. He detested it with a passion. The wounds were still too raw, still too new.

He wanted to yell at her, to shake her and ask her why she deceived him for so long. The biggest lie of them all.

He said it almost softly. "Alisha and Ariel are not biologically mine—two different men, two different affairs. They sent me electronic DNA results after you tore up the paper results. That is the straw that snapped the camel's back, Ashley. Stop grandstanding and stop the melodrama. I never want to see you again. You hear me? Get out of here."

He said the last bit quietly, almost tiredly. "Divorce papers will be served tomorrow. I checked with my lawyer yesterday. Don't play with me on this divorce, Ashley. You better accept my demands, because you have no leg to stand on here. I really... really... really... want to be free of you."

Her eyes widened and she backed away, almost stumbling in her haste to pass all the shocked eyes that were looking at her.

*****

Brandon stood on the back porch after everyone left. Well, everyone but Nadine; she was helping Latoya and Richard clean up.

"Now that was the shortest party on record," his mother said, coming to stand beside him.

His father joined him too. "It was."

"I shouldn't have done it." Brandon pushed his hands in his pockets. "I shouldn't have embarrassed her like that. I shouldn't have said what I said about the children."

He closed his eyes and leaned his head on the wall.

His mother rubbed his back. "You have to admit that she asked for it. She came here to your own party to embarrass you. It was a little shocking to hear about the children, though."

"More than a little," his father sighed. "And you have been bearing this knowledge alone for days."

"Yes," Brandon sighed. "That's right."

"So what have you decided to do?" his mother asked. "I am so put out with Ashley I am inclined to agree with anything you say right now."

Brandon chuckled. "Ah Mom. I am thinking that it's all or nothing. I really don't want to have anything to do with her anymore. So it's either I get full custody of the kids or I completely walk away."

"And we know you are not going to completely walk away," his mother said fearfully. "Right?"

"Right." Brandon nodded.

His parents gave a collective sigh of relief.

"That would have broken our hearts," his father said huskily. "We love them."

"I know," Brandon said. "I do too."

"I wonder if Ashley will still allow us to see them while you are gone," Beatrice whispered.

"Of course," Brandon frowned. "Why not? I was thinking that it is probably best if they stay here with you guys while I am gone. I can't imagine Ashley alone with them for three months, can you?"

Latoya came on the porch with a garbage bag in her hand. "You hungry? We got tons of finger food."

"No," Brandon said, "not hungry at all."

He looked past her to Nadine, who was walking up the steps. "Later we talk, okay?"

He walked Nadine to her car after she said her goodnights to his family.

"Listen," he turned to her, "I am sorry about tonight."

Nadine put her finger on his lips. "No, don't be sorry. I

mean, I can't believe that is what you had gone through with Ashley. It is a small miracle that you can even like another woman again after this."

"Love," Brandon corrected. "I don't just like you."

"You don't know that," Nadine said. "We'll wait until all of this wears off and we'll see if your feelings are not just a rebound thing."

Brandon captured her hands in his and pulled her close. "Okay, that's a plan. I am going away for three months. I'll report back to you then."

Nadine looked at him seriously. "I'll be here waiting through all the stuff, then. I'll be your anchor and your friend."

"Thank you." Brandon hugged her close. "Thank you for being here."

Chapter Eighteen

Three weeks later, Ashley was sitting around her desk, with Damon, her lawyer, on the other side. "This feels like déjà vu," she said meekly.

"Yes, doesn't it?" Damon said. "I can't believe you allowed your husband to file for divorce first; that was foolish. His lawyer says that he's going to sell the house and split the cost, and he wants full custody of the children."

Ashley nodded. "That's only fair. He is leaving me with the business and he's giving me a part of the house sale. That's more than I expected, honestly."

"But," Damon spluttered, "remember what I told you about getting a check every month from him. You won't get that if you give him the children full time."

Ashley twisted her lips. "Leave it, Damon. I won't find a man like Brandon in this world ever again. I wasted my years with him. I played around on him. I treated him with disrespect. The children are not even his."

Damon's mouth opened. "What?"

"You heard me." Ashley hiccupped as tears ran down her cheeks. "I just can't refute whatever it is that Brandon wants. Even now, in divorce, he is showing me some mercy. He is giving me this business so that I can have an income. He is the one that bought this place, paid for my stock..." She looked at his shocked expression. "Yes, I am the stupidest woman on Planet Earth."

Damon closed his mouth with a snap and stammered a bit. "Er...are you interested in visitation with your children?"

"Whatever Brandon says," Ashley said. "The children are with his parents while he is gone. It's three weeks and I haven't got the courage to go and say hello to them. Do I sound like a good mother to you?"

Damon got up. "Okay. Okay. I'll contact Brandon's lawyer today."

"Good." Ashley watched as he walked out of the office. She looked down at her documents. It was ironic, really, her wake-up call had come since that night when she had pushed Brandon to the breaking point and he had blasted her in front of his friends.

When she thought about it, she had to lose him in order to finally come back to her senses. And she had come back down to earth with a bang. She had done some really awful things and she needed God's forgiveness. She needed to go back to basics. She needed to find her way back home.

And this time she was not doing it because she wanted to impress anybody; she wasn't doing it so that she could marry anyone. She was doing it because she needed to change. She knew without a shadow of a doubt that she didn't want to die so selfish and unfeeling.

She was hoping that one day, she could even ask Brandon for forgiveness; he had taken the brunt of her bad behavior over the years. She had done him wrong and she was sorry. Not for the first time a tear slipped down her cheeks. It was followed by a second and a third. It was never too late to change, and she was going to do so one step at a time.

Epilogue

Five years later...

"Why did I agree to this, this year?" Nadine asked Brandon as she stirred a pot on the stove.

Brandon grinned. "You said that you wanted both of our families to meet up this year. That it would be fun, one melting pot of personalities, and that we should all come together with love and laughter. Healing the rifts, et cetera, et cetera."

"Nads," Tara came to the kitchen doorway. "Can I cut the front of Alisha's hair? I think she would look better with bangs."

"No!" both Nadine and Brandon said at the same time.

"Jeesh. You guys are so old fashioned." Tara moved away from the doorway and then indicated the baby in Brandon's hand. "Can I at least hold my nephew while you guys cook?"

Brandon handed over Jacob reluctantly. He was eighteen

months old and looked just like him. Not that it would have been an issue if he hadn't. He trusted Nadine implicitly. They had a partnership, and a friendship that was rock solid. This marriage was so unlike his previous one that he was finding it hard to even remember all the angst that he had with Ashley.

After his three months in Canada he had returned home, gotten divorced from Ashley, and then gotten married to Nadine the year after that.

Eventually, he had started communicating with Ashley again, at Nadine's prompting. Nothing good ever came from being bitter for long, and he was so happy now he couldn't remember with much clarity what it felt like not to be a part of a good partnership.

They had even attended Ashley's wedding a year ago to a minister of the gospel. Brandon could hardly believe that his ex-wife was a first lady.

Sometimes he thought about it and laughed, but the truth was Ashley had changed drastically. She was not the same woman she once was. She saw the girls occasionally, but she still wasn't the world's most maternal person. That much hadn't changed.

He had officially adopted the girls years ago, so that just in case he needed to live abroad, taking them would not be an issue.

"Daddy!" Ariel came to the doorway. "Which one should I wear for the family picture?"

She held up two dresses.

Nadine looked around and then chuckled. "She is a fashionista just like Ashley."

Brandon contemplated the pieces. "I like the lavender."

"Me too." She grinned.

"Mommy, will you be wearing lavender too?"

"Yes," Nadine grinned, "why not? So that our section of the family can match. Tell Alisha."

"Okay," Ariel scampered away.

"So you invited Ashley and her new husband?" Brandon grimaced. "Don't you think he is a bit too, er, holy?"

Nadine threw back her head and laughed.

"He prays at the drop of a hat," Brandon complained, hugging Nadine around her waist.

Nadine chuckled. "He is in a marriage that needs it, Brandon."

Brandon laughed in her neck but he closed his eyes too and prayed silently, "Dear God, thank you for sending this woman into my life. Thank you for my family. Thank you for your blessings. Amen."

THE END

Author's Notes

Dear Reader,

THANK YOU for reading On The Rebound! There is an On The Rebound 2! The excerpt is just a page turn away. I just had to do a story about Ashley and where she ends up and of course Regina is back to create trouble for not just Ashley, who is now a first lady, but the members of the Primrose Hill church where Ashley attends.

If you have comments or suggestions, I welcome them. You can reach me and receive a reply at brenalbar@gmail.com.

You can be among the first to hear when I have special prices and new book releases by signing up for my mailing list. It will take you less than 50 seconds to signup. Signup for my mailing list at brenda-barrett.com

Thanks again. All the best,

Brenda

On The Rebound 2

Church.

She was in church.

Regina sat in the back of the picturesque neat building and looked around with a sense of disbelief. This is what Ashley had unknowingly driven her to, going to church just so that she could see her.

And not any old church either, this church was the epitome of conservativeness. It gave her the creeps. It reminded her of those long ago days when she stayed with her grandparents after her parents divorced. But even then her grandparent's church could not compare to this medieval looking edifice. Everything was minimalist and white—from the gleaming church floors to the material they had covering the podium. The only splash of color was a floral bouquet with some daffodils; their bright yellow blooms were some of the biggest that she had ever seen.

She admired them for a while and then continued to look around in disbelief. The people coordinated with the Spartan decor. From what she could tell from her position in the back row, the women wore long dresses covering their knees...and hats! *Good lord, who still wore those kind of broad brimmed hats in the twenty first century...and blouses buttoned up to their neck?*

And if that was not bad enough everybody had unprocessed hair except for a braided hair or two. No one had on make up or jewelry that she could see.

Even Ashley, Miss fashion plate, sitting at the front of the church was looking plain and unadorned, not even a ring on her finger.

At least she could bring off the plain look, Regina thought admiring her for a while. Ashley did not need makeup or any of that stuff to look pretty. Her hair was natural now and the curly bun she had under the ridiculously frilly blue hat looked curly and thick.

Ashley looked softer somehow; younger if that were possible, and innocent...*no not innocent, pious...that was the word*. She hadn't seen Ashley in person for five years, ever since Ashley's divorce from Brandon Blake.

Regina had kept tabs on her though; even when she had gone to live in the UK and was working as a sports journalist she had hired an investigator to track Ashley.

His reports had been monotonous; Ashley did nothing really remarkable that first year after her divorce. The second year she had started going back to church in earnest and started this mad path she was on to recreate herself into this holy creature. The third year she visited her mother in the States for three months and they seemed to be getting along. The fourth year, Ashley met a guy, Ruel Dennison.

A pastor.

Of all the professions in the world? Regina had been flabbergasted. Ashley really seemed to have a type. She liked straitlaced conservative Christian men. Brandon had been the epitome of straitlaced conservatism and she had thought that Ashley would not have stood a chance with him.

She was wrong then and she was wrong now because this pastor, Ruel Dennison, had married Ashley eleven months ago.

He was even more conservative than Brandon. If her reports from King, the investigator, were right. The pastor was forty years old, a widower with one child, a girl around sixteen who still lived with her grandmother.

The pastor had met Ashley at one of those things that churches have—a convention. It was an event where church folks came together and stroked each others egos, or that was how Regina imagined it having never been to one.

As far as she knew Ashley had not told him about her and their past together and she was backing on the shock factor to get Ashley out of here and away from Ruel Dennison, minister of the gospel. Surely he wouldn't want a wife who had a past like Ashley's. That was her ace card. Ashley made it so easy with her choice of men.

It gave Regina power and she was not afraid to use this ammunition to once more break up Ashley's happy ever after with whatever sucker she had managed to lure into her web. Regina truly believed that Ashley had gotten in over her head. *Surely she couldn't be enjoying this imprisonment in a small hick town in the back of beyond.*

It was possible that the pastor had worked some sort of voodoo on her or given her some sort of magic pill for her to be staying in this place. Surely it was not normal or natural to be this buttoned-up and suppressed. It boggled Regina's mind that Ashley who had just turned thirty-five could enjoy this kind of hemmed in lifestyle.

Regina had to rescue Ashley. She had to do something. Her two months vacation before she joined a local television station as head of their sports department would have to be spent up here in Hicksville trying to get Ashley to see sense once again. And this time she was sure that Ashley would listen...

couldn't read. He embarks on a quest to better himself with an adult learning class. Only to find out that his crush was his teacher. Surely a woman like her would not be interested in an uneducated man from the slums?

Scarlett Promise (Book 5)- After overhearing a whispered conversation that revealed her true parentage, Lisa Barclay ran away from home. She quickly found out that surviving on the gritty streets of Kingston was an uphill battle. Driven by desperation she decides to make some extra money by prostituting herself. Her first customer turns out to be a popular government senator and then to her horror he dies...

Scarlett Bride (Book 6)- Oliver Scarlett loved his job as a missionary doctor in the rarely visited, highly populated village of Kidogo, located in the midlands of the Congo region. He rescued a young village woman from a horrible fate of marrying the old witch doctor by marrying her himself. Now it is time to return home, he has to take his newly acquired bride with him or rescuing her would have been in vain.

Scarlett Heart (Book 7)- After receiving a heart transplant shy librarian Noah Scarlett started to take on character traits that were unlike him. He was going to the gym and loving cherry malt sodas and he kept dreaming of a girl named Charlotte Green...

Rebound Series

On The Rebound - For Better or Worse, Brandon vowed to stay with Ashley, but when worse got too much he moved out and met Nadine. For the first time in years he felt happy, but then Ashley remembered her wedding vows...

On The Rebound 2- Ashley reinvented herself and was now a first lady in a country church in Primrose Hill, but her obsessed ex friend Regina showed up and started digging into the lives of the saints at church. Somebody didn't like Regina's digging. Someone had secrets that were shocking enough to kill for...

Magnolia Sisters

Dear Mystery Guy (Book 1) - Della Gold details her life in a journal dedicated to a mystery guy. But when fascination turns into obsession she finds herself wanting to learn even more about him but in her pursuit of the mystery guy she begins to learn more about herself...

Bad Girl Blues (Book 2) - Brigid Manderson wanted to go to med school but for the time being she was an escort working for her mother, an ex-prostitute. When her latest customer offers her the opportunity of a lifetime would she take it? Or would she choose the harder path and uncertain love with a Christian guy?

Her Mistaken Dreams (Book 3) - Caitlin Denvers dream guy had serious issues. He has a dead wife in his past and he was the main suspect in her murder. Did he really do it? Or did Caitlin for the first time have a mistaken dream?

Just Like Yesterday (Book 4) - Hazel Brown lost six months of memory including the summer that she conceived her son, and had no idea who his father could be. Now that she had the means to fight to get him back from the Deckers, she finds out that the handsome Curtis Decker is willing to share her son with her after all.

New Song Series

Going Solo (Book 1) - Carson Bell, had a lovely voice, a heart of gold, and was no slouch in the looks department. So why did Alice abandon him and their daughter? What did she want after ten years of silence?

Duet on Fire (Book 2) - Ian and Ruby had problems trying to conceive a child. If that wasn't enough, her ex-lover the current pastor of their church wants her back...

Tangled Chords (Book 3) - Xavier Bell, the poor, ugly duckling has made it rich and his looks have been incredibly improved too. Farrah Knight, hotel heiress had cruelly rejected him in the past but now she needed help. Could Xavier forgive and forget?

Broken Harmony(Book 4) - Aaron Lee, wanted the top job in his family company but he had a moral clause to consider just when Alka, his married ex-girlfriend walks back into his life.

A Past Refrain (Book 5) - Jayce had issues with forgetting Haley Greenwald even though he had a new woman in his life. Will he ever be able to shake his love for Haley?

Perfect Melody (Book 6) - Logan Moore had the perfect wife, Melody but his secretary Sabrina was hell bent on breaking up the family. Sabrina wanted Logan whatever the cost and she had a secret about Melody, that could shatter Melody's image to everyone.

The Bancroft Family Series

Homely Girl (Book 0) - April and Taj were opposites in so many ways. He was the cute, athletic boy that everybody wanted to be friends with. She was the overweight, shy, and withdrawn girl. Do April and Taj have a love that can last a lifetime? Or will time and separate paths rip them apart?

Saving Face (Book 1) - Mount Faith University drama begins with a dead president and several suspects including the president in waiting Ryan Bancroft.

Tattered Tiara (Book 2) - Micah Bancroft is targeted by femme fatale Deidra Durkheim. There are also several rape cases to be solved.

Private Dancer (Book 3) - Adrian Bancroft was gutted when he returned to Jamaica and found out that his first and only love Cathy Taylor was a stripper and was literally owned by the menacing drug lord, Nanjo Jones.

Goodbye Lonely (Book 4) - Kylie Bancroft was shy and had to resort to going to confidence classes. How could she win the love of Gareth Beecher, her faculty adviser, a man with a jealous ex-wife in his past and a current mystery surrounding a hand found in his garden?

Practice Run (Book 5) - Marcus Bancroft had many reasons to avoid Mount Faith but Deidra Durkheim was not one of them. Unfortunately, on one of his visits he was the victim of a deliberate hit and run.

Sense of Rumor (Book 6) - Arnella Bancroft was the wild, passionate Bancroft, the creative loner who didn't mind living dangerously; but when a terrible thing happened to her at her friend Tracy's party, it changed her. She found that courting rumors can be devastating and that only the truth could set her free.

A Younger Man (Book 7) - Pastor Vanley Bancroft loved Anita Parkinson despite their fifteen-year age gap, but Anita had a secret, one that she could not reveal to Vanley. To tell him would change his feelings toward her, or force him to give up the ministry that he loved so much.

Just To See Her (Book 8) - Jessica Bancroft had the opportunity to meet her fantasy guy Khaled, he was finally coming to Mount Faith but she had feelings for Clay Reid, a guy who had all the qualities she was looking for. Who would she choose and what about the weird fascination Khaled had for Clay?

The Three Rivers Series

Private Sins (Book 1) - Kelly, the first lady at Three Rivers Church was pregnant for the first elder of her church. Could she keep the secret from her husband and pretend that all was well?

Loving Mr. Wright (Book 2) - Erica saw one last opportunity to ditch her single life when Caleb Wright appeared in her town. He was perfect for her, but what was he hiding?

Unholy Matrimony (Book 3) - Phoebe had a problem,

she was poor and unhappy. Her solution to marry a rich man was derailed along the way with her feelings for Charles Black, the poor guy next door.

If It Ain't Broke (Book 4) - Chris Donahue wanted a place in his child's life. Pinky Black just wanted his love. She also wanted him to forget his obsession with Kelly and love her. That shouldn't be so hard? Should it?

Contemporary Romance/Drama

After The End - Torn between two lovers. Colleen married her high school sweetheart, Isaiah, hoping that they would live happily ever after but life intruded and Isaiah disappeared at sea. She found work with the rich and handsome, Enrique Lopez, as a housekeeper and realized that she couldn't keep him at arms length...

Love Triangle: Three Sides To The Story - George, the husband, Marie, the wife and Karen-the mistress. They all get to tell their side of the story.

The Preacher And The Prostitute - Prostitution and the clergy don't mix. Tell that to ex-prostitute, Maribel, who finds herself in love with the Pastor at her church. Can an ex-prostitute and a pastor have a future together?

New Beginnings - Inner city girl Geneva was offered an opportunity of a lifetime when she found out that her 'real' father was a very wealthy man. Her decision to live uptown meant that she had to leave Froggie, her 'ghetto don,' behind. She also found herself battling with her stepmother and battling her emotions for Justin, a suave up-towner.

Full Circle - After graduating from university, Diana wanted to return to Jamaica to find her siblings. What she didn't foresee was that she would meet Robert Cassidy and that both their pasts would be intertwined, and that disturbing questions would pop up about their parentage, just when they were getting close.

Historical Fiction/Romance

The Empty Hammock - Workaholic, Ana Mendez, fell asleep in a hammock and woke up in the year 1494. It was the time of the Tainos, a time when life seemed simpler, but Ana knew that all of that was about to change.

The Pull Of Freedom - Even in bondage the people, freshly arrived from Africa, considered themselves free. Led by Nanny and Cudjoe the slaves escaped the Simmonds' plantation and went in different directions to forge their destiny in the new country called Jamaica.

Jamaican Comedy (Material contains Jamaican dialect)

Di Taxi Ride And Other Stories - Di Taxi Ride and Other Stories is a collection of twelve witty and fast paced short stories. Each story tells of a unique slice of Jamaican life.

CPSIA information can be obtained
at www.ICGtesting.com
Printed in the USA
LVOW13s1618231216
518585LV00009B/264/P